FRACTURED

VAMPIRE AWAKENINGS, BOOK 6

BRENDA K DAVIES

ALSO FROM THE AUTHOR

Books written under the pen name

Brenda K. Davies

<u>The Alliance Series</u>

Eternally Bound (Book 1)

<u>Hell on Earth Series</u>

Hell on Earth (Book 1)

Coming August 2017

<u>The Road to Hell Series</u>

Good Intentions (Book 1)

Carved (Book 2)

The Road (Book 3)

Into Hell (Book 4)

<u>The Vampire Awakenings Series</u>

Awakened (Book 1)

Destined (Book 2)

Untamed (Book 3)

Enraptured (Book 4)

Undone (Book 5)

Fractured (Book 6)

Historical Romance

A Stolen Heart

Books written under the pen name

Erica Stevens

The Captive Series

Captured (Book 1)

Renegade (Book 2)

Refugee (Book 3)

Salvation (Book 4)

Redemption (Book 5)

Broken (The Captive Series Prequel)

Vengeance (Book 6)

Unbound (Book 7)

The Fire & Ice Series

Frost Burn (Book 1)

Arctic Fire (Book 2)

Scorched Ice (Book 3)

The Kindred Series

Kindred (Book 1)

Ashes (Book 2)

Kindled (Book 3)

Inferno (Book 4)

Phoenix Rising (Book 5)

The Ravening Series

Ravenous (Book 1)

Taken Over (Book 2)

Reclamation (Book 3)

The Survivor Chronicles

Book 1: The Upheaval

Book 2: The Divide

Book 3: The Forsaken

Book 4: The Risen

CHAPTER ONE

"I'D LIKE for you to come with me to my home."

Mia glanced over her shoulder at David as he stood in the doorway of her room. She'd known he was there before he spoke; his inherent woodsy scent of earth and trees was one she'd become increasingly familiar with these past few weeks. She hated that his scent sent shivers of anticipation down her spine, hated that she'd come to rely on his steady presence in her life.

Over the past seven years, the only one she'd had to rely on was herself, and she liked it that way. Or at least she had succeeded in finally convincing herself that was the way she liked it. She didn't want or need someone else in her life. Caring for another only led to heartbreak, and she'd had more than enough of that in her lifetime.

Mia rubbed her hands over her arms before turning back to stare out the window. The snowfall the previous night had left a white coating across the acres of lawn below her. There were castles smaller than this mansion with its sprawling grounds and seemingly endless, rambling rooms. There was plenty of space in this place for the vampires who resided here while they trained to destroy those of their kind who killed humans.

If a purebred vampire came here for training, it was more intense than what the turned vamps experienced. If the purebred passed the training, they would be able to join Ronan's men afterward. The turned vampires who finished their training would be on their own after, but they would be better prepared to spot and destroy the vampires amongst their kind who killed for pleasure.

Mia had been staying at the training compound ever since she'd been rescued by David and the others from the warehouse where she'd been held captive. David and his family had come to the warehouse in search of their loved one, Vicky. Like Mia, Vicky was another purebred vampire who had been imprisoned so that other vampires could pay to dine on their blood.

Goose bumps broke out on her flesh as memories of what had happened in that warehouse danced across her mind. *Easy. Deep breaths*, she told herself.

Closing her eyes, Mia struggled against the panic threatening to pull her into its bleak depths. Before she'd been captured and taken to the warehouse, she'd gotten so much better at controlling the attacks. Ever since she'd been held prisoner, controlling anything had become much more difficult for her again.

Lifting her hand, she pressed her fingertips against the glass in an attempt to center herself in the now. She took another deep breath to fight off the vise grip crushing her chest. Despite the cold glass against her flesh, sweat slid down her nape. Opening her eyes, she took in the serene world before her.

One, two, three, look at the tree, she instructed.

She had no idea when or why she'd ever started doing the rhyming thing when she felt the panic closing in, but for some reason, it helped to calm her. At least it helped sometimes. She focused on the skeletal tree in the center of the lawn with its branches swaying in the breeze. Blobs of snow dropped from its limbs to create dents in the snow on the ground. Keeping her gaze on the tree, breathing slowly in through her nose and out through her mouth, the pressure in her chest gradually eased.

David remained where he was, watching Mia as she gazed

outside. Her shoulders were set rigidly; he detected the increased beat of her heart as she battled the demons haunting her. He would do anything to slaughter those demons for her, but she wouldn't let him get close enough to her to do so.

His gaze ran over her slender form. She'd put on weight since she'd been saved from that building, but her collarbones still stood out against her ivory skin, and the borrowed jeans and sweater she wore hung loosely on her small frame. Vicky had recently cut Mia's sleek, nearly black hair into a bob just below her chin. He'd been surprised Mia had sat and allowed Vicky to do it, but he'd realized that, as Vicky worked, she was careful only to touch Mia's hair and nothing else.

Mia inhaled a jerky breath and lifted her head. In the glass, he saw the powder blue of her eyes before she turned her head to look at him over her shoulder. His breath caught as those eyes landed on him. The gentleness of her features belied the steel rod of strength he knew ran down her spine. With every passing day, she grew lovelier as she healed further.

His pulse quickened as he resisted the impulse to stalk across the room and take her into his arms. Touching her was a sure way to get her to shut down completely on him though. She'd made improvements while here—she was friendlier and not nearly as skittish as when she'd first arrived—but she still went out of her way to avoid anyone's touch.

When they'd discovered her in the warehouse, Mia had thrown herself into his arms. It had been the last time she'd willingly touched anyone for any length of time. He could still recall the feel of her body shaking in his embrace. Her bones had pressed against his palms as he'd held her, trying to ease the terror she radiated.

The image of her in that warehouse, chained to a wall and covered in bite marks, flashed through his mind, causing his hands to fist. Her skin had been raw from those marks, red and swollen to the point where it had hurt her to lie in bed for over a week after she'd been brought here. He'd sat in a chair beside her bed for many nights, listening to her whimpers as she'd tried to get comfortable and wishing he could go back to the warehouse to slaughter every vampire that had been there all over again.

A purebred vampire such as Mia should have healed faster than she had after she was freed, but because of her severe blood loss and the amount of abuse she'd endured, her wounds had lingered for weeks after.

He could still see the faintest hint of bite marks marring the skin around her neck. A human never would have seen them, and maybe most other vampires wouldn't see them anymore, but he did.

His fingers dug into his palms, pulling back skin. He took a deep breath to calm himself as Mia turned to face him. She couldn't see him grappling to maintain his control. It might frighten her, and that was the last thing he ever wanted to do to her.

Over the past few weeks, he'd developed more than a passing suspicion as to what she was to him. He couldn't get her out of his head, the smell of her followed him everywhere, and when he wasn't with her, all he wanted was to see her again and know she was safe.

He'd been around enough mated vampires to recognize the signs of what happened to one when they stumbled across their mate. There had been many women in his life; none of them had ever kept him as riveted as Mia did. He'd be a fool to try to deny the changes in him and his growing need for her. David had considered himself many things over the years, but a fool was not one of them.

If they didn't complete the mating bond, it would only be a matter of time before he lost control of himself. He had to get her to open up to him more, somehow. He had to know for certain if she was his mate or not, and he had to gain her trust. He didn't know how likely that would be as she'd kept herself as untouchable as the clouds in the sky behind her.

But then, maybe his mind would remain fully intact, and he would retain control if the two of them didn't get any closer. His friend Liam hadn't started to completely unravel until after his relationship with Sera became more intimate. He knew Isabelle had tried to push Stefan away, and it had nearly destroyed them both, but he had no idea how much their relationship had progressed before then.

Maybe if he didn't deepen his bond with Mia, he wouldn't go mad. However, it would mean he'd have to leave her in order to put some distance between them, and all he wanted was to feel her against him and know what she tasted like.

Even as he thought about leaving, he knew he wouldn't be able to walk away from her. He had to know she was safe, and though this place had more security than the White House, he trusted no one else to protect her as fiercely as he would.

Which meant it was only a matter of time before he did lose his mind. The looming probability terrified him. He wasn't a control freak by any means; he liked being a little out of control. It was one of the things he loved most about sailing, knowing that even though he had control of the helm, the sea could tear it all away from him in a second. There was something freeing in that knowledge.

However, there was nothing freeing in knowing he could snap and force a bond on Mia that she may not want. He'd rather stake himself before he ever harmed or scared her.

She'd already had far more than her share of crazy and abuse in her life; he didn't want to bring her more, and there was a good possibility he would. Liam had nearly forced the change and the bond on Sera. David had sworn that could never be him, but he was beginning to realize he'd been wrong.

Mia closed her eyes for the briefest of moments to inhale David's crisp scent when he walked over to stand beside her. She knew she should step away from him, yet she found herself unable to resist the warmth he exuded. The last thing she'd planned was to ever get close to another again, but something about him drew her like a fish to a lure. Despite the fact she cursed herself for it, she looked forward to seeing him when they were apart.

Mia focused on the tree in the yard again. Her warm breath created a fog against the glass. Lifting her finger, she drew a small heart within the fog. Tears pricked her eyes as she stared at the heart and the beads of water sliding down it.

"When I was a little girl, my mom and I would leave each other messages on the bathroom mirror," she murmured.

David's breath became trapped in his chest. She'd spoken very little about her family since he'd met her, but he sensed an opening in the walls she'd built around herself. He didn't know how to proceed without having her lock down on him again. For the first time since he was a teen, he felt completely incompetent around a woman again.

Mia placed a single C in the center of the heart.

"What does the C stand for?" he asked.

"My mom's name was Cleo." With a single swipe, she erased the heart. Unfortunately, she couldn't as easily erase the memories of better days long gone by.

"Was? Is your mother dead?"

Mia brushed back a strand of hair falling annoyingly to tickle the corner of her eye. She found herself gazing at the tree in the yard again. A single cardinal landed on one of its branches, fluttering its wings before settling. The vivid red of its color stood out starkly against the snow surrounding it.

"Yes," Mia replied as she remained focused on the cardinal. The striking bird was far more soothing to her than the tree.

"What of your father?"

For a second, David saw sorrow lance through her beautiful eyes.

"Dead," she said flatly.

"Were they both purebreds too?"

"No. They were both turned vampires."

Her clipped tone made him tempted to back off, but his hunger for more knowledge about her far exceeded his hunger for blood.

A stab of disappointment twisted Mia's heart when the cardinal flapped its wings and flew away. She missed its beautiful hue even while she envied its ability to fly so easily away from a place it no longer wished to be. She would flap her wings and fly far from here if she could.

No, I wouldn't, she realized when David shifted beside her.

She didn't want to leave him behind; it was more that she wanted to leave her memories behind. It had taken her a long time to learn it was impossible to escape the past. She'd spent years running from her memories, but they'd doggedly haunted her every step of the way.

"What happened to your parents?" he inquired.

"They were killed in a fire when I was eighteen. I got out. They didn't," she said.

Mia stepped closer to the window as the vise grip bore down on her chest once more. Breathing became difficult and tears burned her eyes.

"I don't know what started it, but it moved so fast. I lost everything that night," she whispered.

"I'm sorry. I can't imagine the pain of that."

Few could and she was grateful for that. No one should have to know what their mother's dying screams sounded like, what it felt like to be helpless to save someone they loved, or the hideous guilt of surviving. It was a burden she wouldn't wish on anyone, not even the pricks who had captured and locked her away.

She still had no idea why she'd survived the fire when her parents had perished. She didn't think she would ever know the answer, but the question plagued her to this day.

"What of your parents?" she inquired.

"My father passed last year. My mother is still alive. Before my dad passed, I saw my parents a few times a year, and I still see my mom. Over the years, I've changed their memories of the encounters and made myself appear older to them."

"I see," she murmured. From her time here, she knew Vicky and Abby's older sister, Isabelle, was mated to Stefan.

"Where did you go after the fire?" David asked.

Mia stepped away from him. His presence may have been relaxing in some ways, but it also brought a sense of closeness that she didn't want to share with another. Her heart clenched when hurt flashed through his eyes. Lifting her hand, she rubbed her breastbone over her heart in order to try to ease the sting. It didn't matter that she didn't want to hurt him. She didn't try to get closer to him again.

"Everywhere and nowhere," she replied.

"Was there someone you could go to for help after?"

"I've had no one for seven years now."

"You're twenty-five?"

"Yes."

He hadn't realized he didn't know her age until then, nor did he know her last name. "What is your last name?"

The distrust in her eyes cut him. He tried to remind himself she'd been through a lot, but he'd thought she'd learned to trust him at least enough to reveal this.

"What is yours?" she asked.

"Perin."

He found himself lost in the soft blue of her eyes while she stared at him from under the thick fringe of her black lashes. Being close to someone was terrifying for her, but for the first time he got the sense she wanted to trust again.

Let her trust me, he silently pleaded.

CHAPTER TWO

"ARDEN," Mia finally answered. "My last name is Arden."

David smiled at her. "I like it."

"Glad you approve," she snorted, but she had to admit that for some bizarre reason she felt happy about revealing it to him. She believed it might have to do with the fact someone *knew* her last name again. She couldn't remember the last time she'd told anyone, nor the last time she'd spoken it aloud. Even the coffee shop where she'd worked before being kidnapped hadn't known her last name, as she'd used a fake ID when she'd applied for the job.

"Mia Arden," she said again and smiled.

It's who I am. How many times had she forgotten that over the years? How many times had she tried to forget it? More times than she could count, that was for sure.

"How old were you when you stopped aging?" David asked.

From being around Liam and Sera's children, he knew that pure-bred vampires didn't know when they would stop aging, but they recognized it instantly when that day arrived. Purebloods had some vampire abilities before then, but they came fully into their powers on the day they reached maturity. Those powers continued to grow over the years, but they never aged another day.

She tilted her head back to look at him. "When I was twenty-two. How old are you?"

"Fifty-two."

Mia turned her attention back to the tree in the yard. "Not so old for a vampire, then."

"No, I'm not," he agreed. "But I intend to live for many more years."

She rested her fingers against the glass once more. "Many do," she murmured, "but many don't end up living for as long as they want. Something always throws a wrench in the works of our plans, doesn't it?"

"Yes," he agreed, unable to tear his eyes away from her profile. Her heart-shaped face, the gentle slope of her nose, and the curve of her full lips all fascinated him. "Were your parents mated?"

"They were. In that way, it was a blessing they both perished in the fire. If only one of them had survived, the other would have destroyed themselves after. I'd have ended up alone anyway."

"You don't have to be alone now."

Didn't she? It was all she'd been for years; she didn't know how to be anything else. She certainly didn't think she had room in her heart, or the courage, to open herself up to another. Not after the fire, and certainly not after her imprisonment.

Mia wrapped her arms around herself. "I don't want to talk about this anymore."

A wave of disappointment crashed over him when she moved farther away. He would give anything to be able to take her into his arms and chase away the anguish haunting her eyes.

It would take time, but she would learn to trust him enough to allow him to hold her. He'd make sure of it. She was already talking to him more now.

Mia lifted her eyes to take in David. At least six feet tall, he had a good nine inches on her five-three height. She had to tip her head back in order to take in the chiseled angles of his cheeks and square jaw. There were many good-looking vamps residing in the house, and some who weren't so handsome, but she found him to be the most striking one of them all.

Most likely broken when he'd still been human, his nose crooked slightly to the side, giving him a rugged air that went perfectly with his tall, athletic build and fresh outdoor scent. He had the long, agile body of a skier.

A body that her fingers itched to touch as desire slid through her belly. It had been a couple years since she'd desired a man, and never so acutely as this. It took all she had not to step closer and press herself against him until no space separated them.

She had no idea where the whim came from. However, once there, it formed an image in her mind that had her fighting against doing exactly that. If she touched him so intimately, she'd probably freeze up or have a panic attack. Both of which would be completely mortifying. He'd already seen her weak and broken in the warehouse, already knew she was a freak who cringed away from any contact with another. She couldn't humiliate herself by giving in to her urge to get closer to him only to turn into a mess.

A strand of his pale blond hair fell to the corner of one of his electric blue eyes. Her gaze dropped to his lips, the upper one stiff while the bottom was fuller. *Biteable*, she decided as she imagined running her tongue over it before drawing it into her mouth and nipping at it.

It wasn't the first time she'd imagined kissing him, and she suspected it wouldn't be the last. She didn't know how much longer she would be able to resist doing it. His touch didn't bother her as much as some of the others, but she still wasn't about to jump into bed with him.

Why does it have to be an all-or-nothing scenario?

Because she knew a kiss wouldn't be enough, not with him. A tremor racked her, and she took another step away in order to put some distance between them. She wasn't so jaded that she didn't recognize David had a good heart, and was a good man, but the idea of getting close to anyone made her want to run screaming for the hills.

"Will you come with me to my home?" David tried to keep his voice level, but he couldn't keep the hope from it.

"What about all the children there? And your friends? Aren't you afraid you'd be putting them in danger by having me there?" Mia inquired.

David didn't know her well—she'd made sure of that—but he did know she wasn't evil. She'd been abused and endured more than she should have in her short life, but she didn't kill humans. The other purebred vampires who had met her would have smelled it on her if she were a killer. Starvation had driven Vicky to accidentally kill a human while she was being held with Mia, but Mia hadn't been pushed to that limit.

"Do you plan to hurt them?" he asked.

"Of course not!" she blurted.

"Then why would they be in danger if you were there?"

"In case you forgot, I was chained to a warehouse wall when you encountered me."

"That's something I could never forget, Mia."

The clench of his jaw, the sheen of red in his blue eyes, and the lethal tone of his voice gave him an air of danger. He'd been nothing but kind to her, but right then she knew he would kill any who threatened her.

She swallowed and tore her attention from him to once again focus on the window. "There might be vamps out there still hunting for purebreds. For *me*. They know what I look like. Taking me to your home could put your family in danger."

"There are thirteen purebred vampires at my home right now. If there are vampires still trying to capture purebreds and feed from them, it won't be just you who brings them to that property. I'd like to see anyone try to hurt someone living there. They'd never survive to regret it."

"Many of the vampires there are young," she said. "Vulnerable."

"Nothing is getting past any of the adults there, trust me on this.

If you feel safer staying here, I understand, but you don't seem happy here."

She didn't think she'd ever be happy anywhere again, but she kept that to herself. Pessimism was as attractive as snot. Besides, what did she know of what her future held? She'd certainly never envisioned being locked up and gorged on by vampires three months ago.

"I think you would like my home," David added.

"There are so many vampires there," she whispered.

"Despite that, it is peaceful." He rested two fingers on her arm, drawing her eyes to him. "And all of those vampires will protect you. I will also make sure they leave you be and keep their distance from you, if you prefer."

"Just what everyone wants, the antisocial house guest," she said with a small laugh.

He smiled at her and slid his fingers around her arm until he held it loosely within his grasp. The silkiness of her skin beneath his hand caused his pulse to spike. His breath caught as a bolt of lust hit him. Gritting his teeth, he shoved it aside. Now was not the time, and if she knew how aroused she made him, she might shut him out.

Vicky said she hadn't endured any sexual abuse during her imprisonment in the warehouse, but that didn't mean Mia had been as fortunate. The thought caused his fangs to prick with the nearly overwhelming drive to kill any who had mistreated her.

Most of those involved in the kidnapping of the purebred vamps were in the process of being hunted down and slaughtered by Ronan and his men. David would love nothing more than to join them—if they agreed to let him help, considering he wasn't purebred or part of Ronan's men—but again that would mean leaving Mia.

As a purebred vamp, she was stronger than him in many ways, yet he'd defend her with his life. He'd also do anything to make her feel safe, even if it meant staying here when he'd much prefer to be back with his friends and family.

He shared no blood relation to Liam and Sera's children, but he considered them all his nieces and nephews, and he loved them all as if they were his blood, perhaps more so. They were closer with each other than many were with their blood family. He missed the laughter and the practical jokes that abounded at home. He missed Liam, Sera, Jack, Doug, and Mike. The last time he'd spent so much time away from his closest friends, he'd been going to college in Pennsylvania while they'd been attending school in Massachusetts.

Then Liam had encountered Sera at a party, their bond had grown, and David had left Pennsylvania behind to help Liam get through the uncertain time. Due to a chance encounter David had with Stefan and Brian years ago, David had known more about what Liam was going through at the time than Liam had. Stefan and Brian hadn't been mated at the time, but they knew what happened when a vampire found their mate.

David could live another thousand years and he'd still never get over how small the world was, as Stefan and Brian were now mated to two of Sera and Liam's children.

Pulling himself out of the past, he focused on Mia again. "Do you wish to stay here?" he asked her.

"I have no idea," she admitted. "I hadn't considered it. I can't return to my apartment, even if I wanted to."

Mia had no idea why she stayed when all the other purebred vamps rescued from the warehouse had already left and were in hiding. Aside from Vicky, she was the only survivor who remained. True, she had nowhere else to go, but Ronan had made sure all the rescued purebreds were taken care of and safe.

She didn't stay because she was afraid of being caught and put back in chains. Most of the vampires who had organized the capture of purebreds and the selling of their blood were dead. The ones who weren't were being hunted and would eventually be caught. Some of the vamps who were still alive knew what she looked like, but they would have no idea where to look for her if Ronan sent her into hiding.

The vamps that may still be looking for her wouldn't be able to track her, unless they had some sort of ability like Brian's. However, if there was another vamp like Brian out there and that vamp had been working for Drake, Ronan believed Drake would have launched an attack against all of them and tried to destroy Ronan and his men.

She believed it had simply been a fluke that her captors had stumbled across her when they did. She hadn't known any of the vampires who had taken her, those who had paid to feed from her, nor any of the other captives before they'd all been held together.

Most of her fellow survivors had chosen where they wanted to go. Ronan would have sent her anywhere in the world she asked him to, as long as he believed it was safe for her there. She could have *finally* gone to Alaska or Finland to see the Northern Lights. She could have lived out her biggest dream, yet she had stayed behind for some reason.

Mia's gaze flicked to David, and she had to admit that maybe she did know why she'd remained, and why she felt so safe. She didn't know him well, but there was a calming, protective vibe from him that led her to believe he would never let anything happen to her again.

Ah damn it, she thought with a sigh.

Just because she'd been celibate the past three years didn't mean she'd sworn off men. She simply didn't want a relationship, and she had a feeling with David it may be deeper than anything she'd experienced with a man before.

Well, she'd actually never had a relationship in her life, not really, and she'd never wanted one. There had been men coming and going, but none that she'd ever considered her boyfriend.

Her parents had loved each other deeply. When she'd still been young, dumb, and full of dreams, she'd yearned to find their kind of love for herself. Then the bleak reality of life had slapped her in the face, and those dreams had gone up like smoke in the wind.

Three years ago, Mia had made a choice to take a step back from the life she'd been living in order to focus more on herself. She'd moved back to Connecticut, where she'd lived with her parents before they'd been killed. She took a job in a coffee shop and rediscovered her love of the stars and space.

She'd sat down and evaluated her life in a way she'd been

avoiding doing since the night her parents died. Then, just when she was beginning to think everything was going to be okay, that she would heal and move on, she'd been ambushed, enslaved, and used as a vampire pincushion.

Mia didn't particularly like anyone, wasn't sure she ever would again, yet she'd stayed because of David.

Okay, maybe she liked David more than a little, and she had to admit that Aiden, Vicky, and Abby were friendly. Vicky understood what Mia had been through in captivity, and even though he could be a bit of an asshole sometimes, Brian had also grown on her. He wasn't nearly as much of an asshole as Lucien, but then Abby had probably tempered Brian's harsher ways a little.

Her gaze lifted to David's full lips, and she almost licked her own as she imagined running her tongue over his in order to taste him. He'd be delicious, she was certain of it. She'd lose herself in him, *to* him, until her hands were on him and his were on her.

She tried not to cringe at the thought of another's hands on her again. Touching her, holding her down....

Her chest clenched as her breath caught in her throat. For a minute, breathing was nearly impossible as she became buried beneath the weight of her memories. She could feel the hands of those who had forcefully drained her blood from her running over her body once more, feel them pinning her onto the cold, hard floor beneath her. Her skin crawled even as anger flared hotly through her at what she considered her defect. She should not lose control of her body every time her past surged through her mind.

One, two, look at your shoes.

Her eyes fell to her sneakers as she labored to breathe. She despised this crushing sense of panic that had occurred often after the fire, when she'd been left all alone in the world. Back then, the panic had been triggered randomly and hit her out of nowhere. She'd spent a lot of time running from it and trying to ignore it. Over the last three years, she'd finally faced it, learned how to handle it better, and gained control of herself.

Now the touch of another, or even the thought of another

touching her, brought the panic forth again. The idea of getting close to anyone turned her into that frightened eighteen-year-old orphan all over again, or it put her back in those chains with the slurping sounds of vampires feeding from her.

She shuddered at the memory of those fangs in her, the weight of their heavy bodies, and their skin on hers....

"Mia?" David rested his hand on her arm when the color drained from her face and her breath wheezed in and out of her. She turned away. "Easy," he murmured as he took his hands from her and held them in the air. "Breathe."

He'd witnessed her having these panic attacks before, but the helpless feeling they created within him didn't ease with each new one. "Breathe," he coaxed until her wheezing eased and some of the color returned to her face. "We can stay here for as long as you want to stay."

We! Mia almost had another meltdown at the comment. Why would he stay with her when she was such a complete train wreck? She didn't sleep at night, she fed only enough to keep going, and panic attacks had become a common occurrence for her once more.

A vampire with panic attacks; who'd ever heard of anything so ridiculous? She felt like a fraud, but then she didn't know why she expected that being a vampire would make her exempt from such things.

There had to be other vampires with issues out there. No one lived for hundreds of years without gaining a few freaking problems along the way.

A bitter laugh escaped her. David went to lower his hands, but she clasped one of them and brought it toward her. Without thinking, she rested his palm against her chest and held it over her racing heart.

Awareness of the man himself caused her nipples to pucker, and a stab of longing speared her belly. He heated her in a way no other man ever had. He made her feel things she'd given up on feeling.

He felt the attraction between them too; she knew he did. Not only had he said 'we,' but he also swayed toward her, and she heard his pulse quicken. Her gaze drifted down his body, her mouth going dry at the delicious sight of him swelling against his jeans. Her heart continued to race, but this time it was from *need.*

If she moved his hand a little to the right, he would be cupping her breast. If he brushed his thumb over her nipple, she'd go limp and collapse.

He'd catch her if she did; she had no doubt of that.

David watched the emotions playing over Mia's expressive face as she tilted her head back to gaze at him. Beneath his palm he felt the staccato beat of her heart. Her tongue darted out to lick briefly over her alluring lips.

Unable to resist tasting those lips for himself, he lowered his head until his mouth brushed against hers. Her eyes widened, watching him. Intent on witnessing every one of her reactions, he ran his tongue over her lips until she whimpered and her lids drooped but didn't cover her eyes completely.

He swept his tongue more demandingly over her mouth. Her legs trembled, her hand tightening on his. Then the breath of her sigh blew over his lips before her eyes closed and she gave herself over to him completely. David's heart thundered in his chest when her lips parted and her tongue stroked his.

Before kissing her, he could have vaguely recalled the taste of strawberries, but now he remembered it clearly as the sweet taste of her enveloped his senses. Lust and something more, something deeper, swamped him as his tongue entwined with hers.

He was done for, he knew it, and right then he happily stepped over the edge to plummet into the abyss of decadence that was Mia alone. He wrapped his arm around her waist and pulled her flush against his chest.

CHAPTER THREE

He knew instantly it had been the wrong thing to do when her pliant body stiffened against him. Her hands flattened on his chest to push him away. She broke the kiss and turned her head away from him while her hands shoved more incessantly against his chest.

Fighting against the need to keep her locked against his body, where she belonged, David gritted his teeth and released her. With a jerky movement, he forced himself to take a step away from her before he frightened her further. She kept her face averted, but he saw the flushed color creeping up her neck. Her shoulders heaved with her rapid inhalations.

Guilt and irritation with himself slithered through him. He knew how skittish she was, how much she disliked being touched, and he understood why after everything she'd endured. He shouldn't have grabbed her like that, but once his mouth had touched hers, he'd been unable to stop himself from taking more.

He'd seen mated vampires battle against the innate part of them that was unleashed when they encountered their mate. Witnessed them nearly lose their minds before the bond was completed. Now he finally *understood* it, as everything in his body rebelled against not being able to draw her closer and claim her as his.

Shit, he thought as he ran a hand through his hair. He was already screwing this up.

"Mia—"

She held her hand up to halt his words before he could become angry with her, or worse, apologize. Her inability to be touched was far from his fault, and if he said he was sorry for kissing her, she may scream.

What is wrong with me?

So many things, she knew. There had been many things wrong with her since the fire. She'd eventually pieced herself back together the best she could in the following years. Then her entire world had been torn completely apart again when she'd been taken. Now all the emotional and physical wounds inflicted on her over the years were torn open and bared to the air. She had no idea how to bandage them up again either.

However, for a second, she'd forgotten all about those wounds and his kiss had brought forth the delicious feeling of belonging within her. She'd lost herself to the heady sensation of his tongue moving over hers in such a demanding and assured way. She'd been kissed more times than she could count over the years, but she'd never been kissed as if she were *everything* for someone. That's the way David had kissed her, and she wanted more of it.

She ached with the desire he stoked to life in her with such ease. There had been a decent amount of men in her past, yet she'd never once contemplated pouncing on one and tearing their clothes from them like she wanted to with David. The idea of removing his clothes and exposing what she knew had to be a magnificent body, enticed her as much as the idea of him touching her, or of him being on top of her, made her inwardly cringe.

Just being held against his chest for that brief time made her recall all those vampires sitting on top of her as they feasted from her.

Her stomach turned over as the squeezing sensation returned to her chest. She could feel their flesh rubbing against hers as they laughed at her and with each other. The fear that had come with the increasing weakness seeping through her body as they drained her blood threatened to overwhelm her.

She'd fought them so hard in the beginning, but as time passed the fight went steadily out of her. By the end of her captivity, she'd been ready for them to finally drain her until there was nothing left. To finally get the inevitable *over with.*

She despised herself for those times when she had lain there praying for it all to end. She should have continued to fight, but instead she'd been so weak and pitiful. Now with her newfound aversion to touching another, she knew she was still weak and pitiful.

She hugged her stomach as she stepped farther away from David. "I'm a disaster," she told him. "You'd do better to stay away from me."

"You've been through a lot."

She hated his understanding almost as much as she hated her memories. "I'm not a project for you to fix. I can do that on my own. I have before."

"But you don't have to do it alone anymore." David studied her eyes when her gaze finally came back to him. He saw wariness there, but he also saw a burgeoning anger he found refreshing. Anger was far better than the desolation on her face seconds before.

"Are you going to do it with me?" she snapped.

"Yes."

His simple answer melted away some of her annoyance with him as she gazed up at him. "No one ever does something for nothing. Why would you want to help me?"

"Because everyone needs someone to care for them. I've been fortunate in my life to have many who care for me. You deserve the same."

"You don't know that. What if I don't deserve it? You know nothing about me. For all you know I could be a vindictive bitch who has deserved everything that's happened to me."

"I don't believe that. At the very least, you're not a killer."

She alternated between glaring at him and wanting to throw her arms around him. To have someone so stubbornly sure of her was something she hadn't experienced since her parents passed. She'd honestly believed she never would again. To experience it now, when she was about as fucked up as one could get, seemed even crueler and more unfair to her than being shackled to a wall had been.

"Can't you tell I'm broken?" she demanded. "I can't stand anyone touching me!"

"You handled me touching you until I pushed you too far."

"Freaking out because someone you're enjoying kissing tries to get closer to you is *not* normal."

"It wasn't normal that I was turned into a vampire because a female vamp became obsessed with my best friend," David replied. "When Liam didn't follow after her, she decided to turn his friends in the hopes she would get him to fall in line with her. That's about as far from normal as it gets. I didn't have a clue about the paranormal being real when my transformation occurred. Vampires were for horror movies, not reality. Life's not normal. Shit happens. We all work through it."

"Is that so, Dr. Phil?"

The frustrating man smiled at her.

"That's so," David replied.

Mia opened her mouth to respond, but closed it again when she heard voices coming down the hall. She turned to the door as Abby and Vicky appeared, the twins smiling as they waved at her and David. Each of them had their light blonde hair pulled into a ponytail and towels draped around their shoulders.

Though they were identical, and Vicky had regained the weight she'd lost when she'd been imprisoned, Mia could tell the difference between the sisters. Abby proudly wore the bite marks her mate, Brian, left on her. Vicky's neck was unblemished; the wounds she'd sustained while held prisoner had vanished from her skin. If the sisters were wearing turtlenecks, Mia would have no idea which was which.

"Ready for some training, Mia?" Abby asked, her green eyes

sparkling when they went from her to David. Her smile widened as she gazed at him.

Mia could feel the love they all had for one another in the smiles they exchanged and the easy comfort with which they all interacted. It was a love she'd witnessed often since being here with them.

She couldn't help but feel a little jealous of it. No one had looked at her like that, or cared for her in such an open way, in years. Until she'd met them, she hadn't realized how much she missed that kind of simple, easy love.

"David," Abby greeted.

"Mary Kate, Ashley," he replied with a smirk.

Vicky and Abby's mouths parted before they exchanged disbelieving looks. "Did Moe just call us the Olsen twins?" Vicky demanded.

"I think he did," Abby replied. "And you see David as Moe? That would mean he'd be the leader of the Stooges."

"You're right, that's definitely Mike. Larry, then?"

"I was thinking more along the lines of Curly."

"Really?" Vicky asked. "I always kind of saw Doug as Curly."

Abby tapped her finger against her chin. "I can see that."

The two of them grinned at each other before turning their mischievous looks on David. "Shemp," they said at the same time. "He's definitely Shemp."

"Get out of here before I kick both your asses," David said.

Mia heard the amusement in his voice when he issued this threat.

Vicky waved her fingers at him. "Oooh, we're scared."

"Go," David said.

"We were going anyway," Vicky retorted. "We'll see you in the gym, Mia."

"I'll be there," she replied, watching as the sisters strolled away.

"See you later, Shemp!" they called down the hall behind them.

Mia bit on her bottom lip to keep from laughing as David scowled after them. She'd come to learn that all of Liam and Sera's ten children affectionately referred to David and his friends as the Stooges. David acted like it bothered him, but she had a feeling he secretly loved it as much as he loved the children he'd helped to raise.

"I should go," she said and turned away from David.

She may not like to be touched, but since her capture, she'd realized she had to be able to defend herself better. Those vamps had taken her unawares before; it would *not* happen again. If someone jumped her now, she would be able to defend herself, and she would have a weapon with her. Before she'd never considered carrying a stake or crossbow with her, but now there wasn't a time she was without one.

David held his hand out to stop her, careful not to touch her as she froze inches away from his fingers. He tried not to let her aversion bother him, but a pang tugged at his heart when she gazed nervously at his palm.

"Think about coming to my home with me," he said. "There are others there who would like to meet you. It will also be safe, and it is far more inviting than this place."

"And why would any of them like to meet me?" she inquired.

David's gaze unwaveringly held hers. The ravenous gleam in his eyes made her toes curl and her fingers instinctively rise to her lips. They were still swollen from his kiss. The taste of him lingered on her mouth; he'd tasted like he smelled, of pine and fresh air. His kiss had only increased her hunger for him instead of satisfying it in any way.

"I think you know why," he said.

Dropping his hand, he turned away from her and walked out of the room. Mia's eyes remained latched onto his broad shoulders until he vanished from view. *What does that mean?*

She had a sneaking suspicion she already knew the answer to that question. She'd seen her parents; she knew the stories of mated vampires and the attraction that pulled them toward each other. Not one of the men who had wandered through her life had left her aching for more the way David did.

The possibility of a mate was something she simply couldn't consider right now, no matter how much her body and mind were trying to tell her it could be David. She'd spent her first eighteen years dreaming of the day she found her mate. Then she'd come to know that life was a fickle bitch, and the years since the fire had convinced her she would never find her mate or know love again.

It was the cruelest twist of fate that she might have stumbled across her mate now, when so much of her had died in that fire, and the rest of her had been shredded while wearing chains.

CHAPTER FOUR

MIA REPEATEDLY PUMMELED the punching bag as she attempted to beat the stuffing out of it. Maybe, just maybe, she could exorcise herself of some of her own demons if she hit it hard enough. Maybe she could be normal again.

Okay, that was hoping for too much from a punching bag, but it was worth a try. Plus, Lucien was holding the bag, and every time he grunted, she felt a jolt of satisfaction. She drove her fists so violently into it that she pushed him back a step. Lucien's head popped out from behind the bag, his raven-colored eyes narrowed on her.

"What has you in a mood?" he inquired as he released the bag to run a hand through his sandy blond hair. His hair stood up in tousled spikes around his handsome face when he was done with it.

"Nothing," she replied and stepped away from the bag.

"Must be that time of the month," he grumbled.

Mia glowered at him and instinctively moved farther away when he strode by her toward the bench on the side wall. The loose-fitting sweats he wore hung low on his hips. Her gaze ran over the chiseled muscles of his back and sides as they flexed with every step he took.

The sweat beading on his smooth skin caused it to shine. She appreciated his stunning physique, yet the idea of running her fingers over his body made her inwardly recoil.

At one time, after the fire, she might have screwed Lucien to simply try to forget for a bit. However, she'd come to realize that though she may forget her loss for a brief period of time, she always remembered afterward, and she'd always been left bereft once more. Still, sometimes it had been nice to be close to someone for a bit. To make believe they cared for her when she knew they didn't, and she'd honestly never cared for them either.

Now all she wanted was her distance from everyone, except….

Her eyes went to where David stood with Vicky and her older brother, Aiden. The three of them were taking turns sparring with each other as they danced around the mat. Her gaze hungrily drank in the bunch and flow of his lean muscles as he moved with easy grace. She licked her lips, savoring the taste of him. The idea of running her fingers over his body, of feeling those muscles flowing beneath her, didn't make her recoil at all; instead, her body heated, and her pulse picked up.

A hand brushing against her arm caused her to nearly leap out of her skin. The unnatural sensation of someone's flesh sliding over hers made her breath lurch. She bit on her bottom lip to suppress the scream surging up her throat.

"Sorry," a young turned vampire said to her before walking away.

Her skin crawled from the lingering effects of his touch, memories of her imprisonment slithering forth like a snake from its den.

One, two, three, four, look at the door.

Her gaze latched onto the door leading out of the gym. She took a few steadying breaths as she took in the lock, the hinges, the glass window. Some of the constriction in her chest eased as her eyes slid closed. The warmth of someone near her made her body prickle uncomfortably, and she knew Lucien had returned. She'd worked with him in training often enough to recognize his spiced scent.

Then she felt another presence, and the aroma of the outdoors filled her nose. Opening her eyes, she turned her head to find David standing nearby. "Are you okay?" he inquired.

She forced a smile as the constriction in her chest eased. "Fine," she replied. *Now that you're here*. But she kept that to herself. Things were already strange enough between them.

Her attention was drawn to Brian, Abby's mate, when he stepped onto the mat and walked over to where Abby was jumping rope. Abby stopped before he reached her; a smile spread across her mouth as she stepped closer to him and leaned against his side. The love pouring from the mated pair caused Mia's breath to hitch. Brian turned his head into Abby's hair, kissing her tenderly before bending to lift her into his arms. Abby grinned as he carried her from the room.

Mia knew that for the two of them the rest of the world had ceased to exist. She had witnessed the same thing often enough with her parents while growing up. A simple touch between the two of them would make them forget she was in the room. She'd never doubted her parents' love for her. She'd known they would die for her as quickly as they would die for each other, but in those private moments between them, she'd simply been a bystander.

She missed being that bystander. She missed *them*.

Tears burned her eyes as fresh sorrow swelled within her. It had been seven years since she'd lost them. There were times when it felt like it *had* been seven years, if not more. Then there were times, like now, when it felt as if only minutes had passed. Times when the grief became so consuming she once again stood in the snow, the flames snapping high into the air as everything she'd ever loved crumpled before her.

"I've had enough for today." Mia didn't look at Lucien or David before turning and walking out of the gym.

David watched her go with a heavy heart. The sadness in her eyes, the defeated slope to her shoulders, was more than he could stand.

"Aren't you going after her?" Aiden asked.

He glanced over his shoulder at where Aiden stood only a foot away from him. Aiden's leaf green eyes were unrelenting as they held his. His once curly black hair had been shaved down to stubble once Aiden started his training with Ronan's men.

Though there were other vamps training under Lucien's supervision, Aiden was the only purebred amongst them. He was also the only one who would make it into Ronan's inner circle if he passed his training. From what he'd learned, David knew most purebred vampires didn't pass the extensive training, but he had no doubt Aiden would succeed.

"I'm not sure she wants company right now," David replied.

"She does," Aiden said firmly.

"And how do you know that?"

"Because I'm not a fucking idiot, Shemp."

Behind Aiden's shoulder, Vicky giggled and grinned at him as she waved. No matter how much he loved them, there were times he contemplated calling Liam to let him know he was down one kid. This was one of those times. He knew the nickname would change and he would eventually become Moe or Larry again depending on the mood of the kids, but Shemp was really grating on his nerves for some reason when it never had before.

"All you Byrne kids are assholes," David told them.

"To be fair, Kyle and Cassidy are too young to be assholes already, but we'll get them there," Aiden replied. "Now if I were you, I'd get going. A few of the turned vampires here think Mia's hot. You might miss your chance with her if you wait too long."

David had heard the expression "blow your top" before, but he'd never truly understood it until Aiden's words caused his fangs to elongate as a haze of red instantly shaded his vision. He'd tear the throat out of the first one he heard call her "hot," or who dared to get close to her. *No one* would take her away from him.

Aiden took a step back and held up his hands in a pacifying gesture. "Easy, David," he coaxed.

His words barely penetrated the angry buzzing in David's head as he turned on his heel and stalked after Mia.

"Why did you say that to him?" he heard Vicky ask her brother.

"I thought a little nudge might do him some good. They keep dancing around each other," Aiden replied.

"He almost tore your head off because of that 'little nudge.' You know better than to mess with a vampire during this time."

"I know better about a lot of things I do, but I still do them," Aiden stated. "Besides, it worked, didn't it? He's going after her."

"You're all idiots," Lucien chimed in.

Whatever else they said was lost to David as he stepped out of the gym. Following Mia's inherent rose scent, he made his way down the hall to the outside door. The cold air slapped him in the face when he pushed the door open. The wind blowing across the ground lifted the snow until it swirled in the air around him in dancing flakes as he walked.

He stopped outside the door to the main house, frowning as he sniffed at the air. He turned away from the door when he realized Mia hadn't gone back inside. Following her scent, he walked around the building toward the side yard.

He found her standing beneath the boughs of the tree she could see from her room. As he walked closer to it, he realized that it was a large maple. Mia stared into the tree as a cardinal hopped through the numerous branches.

"You know they say a cardinal is the representative of a loved one coming to visit you," Mia said when David stepped beside her. She'd heard his footsteps in the snow, but she would have known he was there before she'd heard him. Her skin had become electrified the second he'd turned the corner of the mansion.

David watched the bird as it continued to descend, moving through the branches as if it were enticed by her too. And why wouldn't it be? Her soul may be battered, but the strength of it radiated from her. He had a feeling she didn't know how strong she truly was.

"I've heard that," he replied.

"My mother loved birds. If anyone were to come back for a visit, it would be her. Or with as close as they were, maybe my parents hitched a ride on the same bird."

A wistful smile tugged at the corners of her lips as the cardinal stopped a few feet above her. It tilted its head back and forth, studying her. David had never put much credence into the idea, but with the way the cardinal watched her, he started to rethink his stance on the whole thing.

"I've known enough mated vampires to believe that could be true," he admitted.

"Growing up around the kind of love they had, I used to dream of finding a mate for myself one day. I'd always known I could go my entire life without meeting my mate, but I'd also known it was possible he was out there, waiting for me. I would have waited for him forever. Then the fire tore my world apart, and I no longer dreamed of anything. Dreams are for children. I stopped being a child that night."

David studied her profile as she watched the bird moving ever lower. The cold had caused a redness to creep across the cheeks of her heart-shaped face. Her full mouth pursed as her head tilted to the other side while she watched the bird. The small point to her chin gave her an air of determination.

He shoved his hands into the pockets of his sweats to keep from brushing the hair back from her face when the wind blew it forward. "Where did you go after the fire?" he asked.

"Everywhere and nowhere," she replied. "I had nowhere to go. No one to turn to. My parents had some vampire friends over the years, but not many. They had a falling out with a man who was a close friend of theirs shortly after we moved into the house that caught on fire. They lost contact with others over time, and two were killed by hunters."

Mia pushed back her hair before continuing. "At first, I was too devastated after the fire to think clearly, and I found myself wandering the streets of Hartford. To this day, I still have no memory of how I got to the city. We lived a good half hour away from Hartford, and when I finally became aware of my surroundings, I didn't have a car with me.

"I had no money, no job, no shelter. I was a purebred vampire, stronger than most recently turned vamps already, but I hadn't fully matured or completely come into my abilities at that time. If I'd been older, I could have used my ability for mind control to get an apartment, but I didn't have enough skill with it at the time to keep up the charade.

"My mind control would sometimes last for a week or two on a human. At other times, only a day or an hour. Maybe I could have kept doing it to someone, but who knows what that kind of continued manipulation to the human mind does over time. I wasn't willing to take the chance of inflicting permanent damage on someone."

"I don't blame you," David said when she stopped speaking.

"After my mind control wore off, and the people I'd been manipulating realized I didn't belong in that hotel room or apartment, I'd find myself back on the streets. In the beginning, I was so heartbroken and confused that I really didn't care about having a place to stay or anything of my own. I didn't know what to do or how to handle everything that had happened to me. It was also when the panic attacks first started," she admitted in a shamed whisper.

David's fingers flexed as he resisted resting his hand on her shoulder to comfort her. She would jerk away though, move farther away from him and possibly retreat inside. This was the most she'd ever opened up to him; he couldn't do anything to push her away. However, not being able to do anything for her was the most frustrating experience of his life.

"I struggled to survive with the other street kids, and there were a lot of them. Too many," Mia continued. "The emptiness in their eyes, what they had to do to survive, to eat, broke my heart. No matter how many times I moved, or the different cities I went to, that emptiness and the circumstances for those kids were always the same. I was different than they were, yet I also fit in with them and didn't feel quite so alone when I was with them.

"My vampire abilities may not have been honed back then, but I was far more fortunate than those kids were. I was faster and stronger. I didn't have to do the things those humans did to survive. I didn't get beat up or raped. I watched out for more than a few of them and defended them, but I also fed on them. If you really want to feel like a piece of shit, feed from someone who's weaker and has it worse than you. It's sobering and awful."

"You did what you had to do to survive," David said.

"We all do that. It doesn't mean we always have to like it, or that it's right in any way."

"No, but it also doesn't mean we have to continuously beat ourselves up over it afterward."

"Perhaps." Her eyes were haunted when she turned toward him. "I've never killed another."

"I've killed other vampires."

"Do you regret it?"

"Not a single one," he bit out with clenched teeth. Some of the vampires he'd destroyed had been in that warehouse holding her captive. "I'd gladly kill every one of them again, especially the ones who hurt you."

Mia's head tilted to the side as red flashed through David's eyes. Always so patient and kind with her, she sometimes forgot how lethal he could be. She'd witnessed his brutality within the warehouse when he'd helped take down her captors with ruthless efficiency. Unlike the vampires who had held her captive, his ability to be so savage intrigued her, or perhaps it was just him who piqued her curiosity so much.

"You believe yourself to be my mate."

Never one to beat around the bush, she figured she'd get it out in the open; she saw no reason to continue to tiptoe around one another. His eyes widened at her blunt words, his lips pressed together as his hands jerked in his pockets. He was trying to keep from grabbing her, she realized.

"I do." He focused on her face to pick out every minute detail of her reaction to his words, but she remained expressionless. "No woman has ever fascinated me the way you do. I've never wanted to protect and cherish one like I do you. I can't get you out of my head."

Mia tilted her head to the side as anguish twisted in her chest and tears burned her throat. He was too good of a man; he deserved someone far better than her. He deserved someone who could love him and hold him. She didn't know if she had it in her to love again, or if she would ever be able to accept the touch of another.

"I'm worse than a shattered mirror. You can't put me back together," she said.

"You're not shattered. Fractured maybe, but not shattered."

Mia couldn't stop her snort of laughter when he smiled teasingly at her while he spoke.

"Besides," he continued, "I never said I wanted to put you back together."

"You like weak women, then?" Mia demanded, incensed that he might think of her that way, and worse, that he wanted her to stay that way. "Or do you have a savior complex?"

David blinked at her. "God, no. What's the fun in a weak woman? I'm no one's savior, and you don't need one. If you think you're weak, Mia, then you haven't been paying attention these last few weeks. There was a time when you wouldn't leave your room, or go anywhere near the others. Now you're training to fight back against anyone who threatens you. You may not realize it yet, but you're already working toward making yourself whole again. You're saving yourself."

Mia didn't know how to respond; he'd taken all sense of the English language away from her with those words. She opened her mouth, then closed it again. He considered her strong. That realization pleased her more than she ever would have believed possible.

"I haven't felt whole since the day I stood in my front yard and watched my home collapse," she admitted in a ragged whisper as a single tear slid down her cheek.

"You've been through a lot between losing your parents and being held captive for three months," he said. He couldn't stop his fangs from extending over the reminder of how long she'd endured the abuse of those bastards. "No one comes out of that the same as they were before. You're being too tough on yourself."

"Or maybe I'm smart enough to realize I'll never be the same again, and you deserve better for a mate than someone who is a borderline basket case."

Pulling one of his hands free of his pockets, he rested his palm against her chilled cheek and wiped away the tear. She twitched but didn't move away from him. "You're already allowing me to touch you more than you ever did before."

"I'm not sure if you're the most understanding man I've ever met, or just crazy," she said.

"Maybe I'm a bit of both."

"Maybe," she agreed and stepped away from him.

David lowered his hand back to his side. "Do you believe I'm your mate?"

Her head tipped back as she contemplated his question. She couldn't deny her intense attraction to him. David made her fingers itch to touch him, and her body to melt in a way she hadn't realized it could. Despite her dislike of being touched, she craved knowing what it would feel like to have him deep within her, taking possession of her body.

But that would mean flesh against flesh, and touching more deeply than a simple hand on a face, or lips against lips. The chill racing down her spine had nothing to do with the December wind whipping around them and everything to do with allowing herself to be vulnerable in such a way again.

"I can't deny there is a pull between us," she finally admitted. "But for your sake, I really hope I'm not your mate."

She didn't wait to hear what he would say before turning on her heel and walking back to the main house. The monstrous building loomed high, casting a shadow over her and blocking out the afternoon sun. She couldn't shake the ridiculous notion that it wanted to devour her.

David had been right before; she wasn't happy here. The place would have a cold air to it even in August. With the leaves off the trees and the snow blanketing the ground, the mansion felt frigid and menacing. There was an austerity to it that made her skin crawl, but she'd chosen to remain, and she had nowhere else to go.

Or did she? She recalled David's offer from earlier about his home, and she felt his eyes boring into the back of her head as she walked inside.

CHAPTER FIVE

"SHE'S PLAYING HARD TO GET," Liam said through the phone.

"She's not playing," David replied as he ran a hand through his hair, tugging on it until it stood up as he paced back and forth in his room.

His eyes ran over the red walls surrounding him, his upper lip curling back in distaste. The house he shared with Jack, Doug, and Mike may not be the best decorated or most well-kept in the world—it was old and a definite bachelor pad—but this red everywhere made him want to tear the wallpaper down with his bare hands.

"She's had a difficult time of it for seven years now," he said to Liam.

"So you said," Liam replied. "But you can get her through it."

"Can I? Because I'm not so sure about that."

"Better you than Jack. He would have thrown up his hands and walked away by now."

David chuckled. "No, not even Jack would have walked away from this... this *draw* I feel to her."

Liam became silent and David could practically hear the wheels spinning in his friend's head. "You think she's your mate," Liam finally stated.

"Yes, I suspect she is," David admitted.

"Then you *will* get her through this."

"How?"

"Just be there. It's all you can do. From what you've said it sounds like she's already grown to trust you more."

"I think so."

"Then let her come to you in her own way and own time. If she is your mate, as a vampire, she won't be able to resist the pull between you for long either."

David stopped pacing to stare at the golden mirror across from him, another thing he would have heaved out of this house if it were his. "You're right," he said.

"I usually am," Liam replied.

"Not often that I can recall."

Liam laughed, and David heard the cushions sink as he plopped himself onto a couch. "Maybe try taking her on a date or something, romance her."

"Sure, it will be really romantic to be blindfolded so we can leave this place and then have someone else drive us around like we're teenagers. I didn't like that when I was fourteen and going on my first date."

"That's because your mom drove you, and she told you and your date that your braces would lock together if the two of you kissed."

"That's right, she did." With a fond smile, David recalled the human memory he'd forgotten until then. "And we both believed her."

"No kiss for you that day."

"No kiss for me until those damn things came off a year later," David muttered. "I doubt it would be any more fun now to have someone driving us around on a date."

"Probably not," Liam agreed. "You'll figure something out. Are you going to be able to return home soon?"

"I don't know," he admitted. "I asked Mia if she would come with me, but I think it may be too much for her right now."

"It most likely would be with the zoo we have here. Don't push her on that."

David wouldn't push her to do anything she wasn't ready for, but he missed his home. Years ago he could have set out and gone his own way, but he'd realized when he'd broken off to go to college in Pennsylvania that he was happiest among his friends who were family to him. He'd traveled the world, seen the sights, and done his fair share of partying over the years, but none of it made him feel as content as when he was in his own bed.

"I won't," he muttered. "How did you get through this with Sera?"

"Not well, at least not toward the end before our bond was completed, if you remember."

"I do. If I hurt Mia in any way, if I push too fast or scare her, she'll bolt, connection between us or not."

"I'd like to say to not do those things, but I never thought I'd do any of the things to Sera that I did," Liam said. "The difference is you know what this could be between the two of you. I didn't. Work with that knowledge, don't try to deny it, and move slow. If you don't progress through some of the steps for a while, you'll be better able to control yourself."

"Yeah," David agreed as a high-pitched squeal sounded through the phone. "Who was that?"

"Mandy and Jill are visiting Emma. Mandy's getting married in the spring, and they're working on planning things. Jill just shoved Cassidy into the pool."

"I thought you shut the pool down."

"I did. Cassidy's flopping around on the cover like a fish on land."

David laughed and sat on the edge of the bed. "Big bad purebred vampire getting shoved around by a human."

"She won't live it down either. Willow, Julian, and Kyle all witnessed it."

No, Cassidy would never live that down. "How is everyone else?"

"They're all good. How are my kids?"

"Aiden's training is going well, and I've never seen Abby happier."

"Vicky?"

"She's doing better. There's still a sadness in her that was never there before. She's strong though, always has been. I wouldn't be surprised if she doesn't try to join Ronan's group with Aiden."

"I'll keep that to myself until it happens. Sera's already worried enough about what Aiden is doing without thinking her daughter may be contemplating the same thing. It would be nice if they made it home for Christmas. And you."

"It would."

He didn't think that was likely, but he wasn't about to tell Liam that in case things changed.

He talked with Liam for a few more minutes before setting the red phone back on its cradle. This may be the ugliest room in the place, but it was also one of the few with a phone in it, and getting cell reception had proven impossible.

Rising to his feet, he stalked out of the room. He had to move, to feel fresh air or do something before he started tearing the wallpaper down. He stood in the hallway, his gaze on the closed door of Mia's room beside his. Instead of going toward it, he forced himself to turn the other way. After their discussion earlier, she needed her space, and he would give it to her.

Stepping out of the hallway, the sound of the TV pulled him toward the only room with a television in it. He found Vicky lounging on the couch with her legs draped over one of its arms. Her feet swung back and forth as she watched the news.

"Anything good going on in the world?" he asked her.

"Is there ever?" she replied without looking at him.

"No."

She pulled her feet back when he walked over to perch on the arm of the couch. His mind drifted to Mia as images of government officials flashed by on the screen. There had to be something he could do to make her smile, to bring her some happiness.

The nudge of Vicky's toe in his side pulled him from his thoughts. "You ever been to the center of the maze out back?" she asked.

"A few times," he replied.

"It's pretty romantic."

He couldn't help but smile even as he shook his head at her. "Playing Cupid now?"

"That's Abby's department. I'm just saying it's really pretty out there. You're the one who jumped to Cupid."

"So I did," he turned his attention back to the TV. "I'm pretty sure that's also become Brian and Abby's spot."

"True." Vicky nudged him with her toe again. He arched an eyebrow at her when he turned to look at her. "There's a lake out behind the maze. I discovered it last week. The hedges for the maze keep it blocked out, and I think most don't know it's there because they're always focused on the maze. It's really pretty and peaceful."

"I'm sure it is."

Vicky returned to staring at the TV. "Thought I'd let you know about it."

He rested his hand on her calf, drawing her attention back to him. "Thank you."

She grinned at him and put her foot into his side below his ribs. "Don't mention it," she replied, then shoved him off the arm of the couch. "See you later, Shemp."

"Just when I think one of you kids might not be such an asshole, you prove me wrong."

Vicky's laughter followed him out of the room.

CHAPTER SIX

"It's beautiful," Mia breathed as she gazed at the pristine lake water. The fresh snowfall early this morning clung to the branches of the willows dipping toward the water. The white-covered world around them reflected in the dark blue water in such a way that it was almost as if she gazed into a mirror image of their world.

"It is," David agreed.

She looked at him as he stood beside the lake with his hands shoved into his coat pockets. The wind had tousled his hair in a boyish way. His eyes were the color of a robin's egg in the early morning sun filtering over him. Her fingernails dug into her palms as she resisted reaching out to stroke the dark blond stubble lining his jaw.

She wanted to be able to melt against him, to give him everything she knew he deserved from a woman. To take the pleasure she knew he could give to her. His kiss had nearly set her blood on fire. What he could do to her with his hands and tongue might just make her spontaneously combust, *if* she didn't have a panic attack first. That *if* was more like a guarantee though.

After their conversation about mates yesterday, he'd stayed away from her for the rest of the day and night. It had been the longest she'd gone without seeing him since he'd pulled her out of that warehouse. She'd spent all night tossing and turning with the fear that he'd realized she was right, that he deserved better than her for a mate.

There had been numerous nights, after she'd first been freed, when the sound of her crying out from her nightmares had woken David and drawn him into her room. Unwilling to be alone, she hadn't complained when he'd settled into a chair beside her bed and sat with her for the rest of the night.

Most times, she never fell back asleep and would watch him as he watched her, afraid that if she took her eyes off him for one second, he'd vanish. She never would have made it through those nights, and the many that had followed, without him. Perhaps she should have wondered then if there was something more between them than a burgeoning sort of friendship, but she hadn't been able to think past getting through one minute at a time.

She hadn't realized how much he'd come to mean to her until she'd gone nearly a day without seeing him. She'd repeatedly cursed herself for being such an emotional wreck while she'd trudged her way into the shower that morning. Convinced he'd decided to go back home without her and find a normal woman, she'd felt as if her heart were made of lead while she dressed. To her dismay, she'd realized how much she would miss him and had already come to rely on him.

Then she'd heard a knock on her door. She'd practically tripped over her own feet to answer it when she caught his scent on the other side. Breathless when she'd flung the door open, she'd nearly thrown herself into his arms before he could ask her to go for a walk. She'd somehow managed to compose herself enough to make it to the lake with him, but that need for more of him was growing within her again.

Without thinking, she stepped closer to him, drawing his attention to her. In his eyes, she saw the same desperate want that churned within her. Lines crinkled the edges of his eyes as his jaw locked.

"Let's take a walk around the lake," he suggested.

Mia bit her bottom lip as she tried to control the ache in her body while she gazed at him. "Yes," she managed to choke out.

He made a move as if to take hold of her hand before lowering his hand to his side. Feeling beat down, Mia kicked her feet through the thin layer of powdery snow. She kept her focus on her borrowed boots, which were a size too big on her, as they made their way leisurely around the lake.

Lifting her head, she gazed at the trees. No breeze stirred their white-coated limbs. The birds didn't even chirrup, and nothing moved through the forest while they walked. A peaceful hush hung over the world around them.

"It's like we're the only ones who exist here," she murmured. "As if time has stood completely still."

David tore his gaze away from her to take in their surroundings. "It does seem that way."

"I know it's not your home, but do you like it here?" she asked.

"At the training facility or by this lake?"

She smiled as she tipped back her head to look at him. "The training facility."

David hesitated as he debated how to answer her question. He didn't want her to possibly feel bad about him still being there if he told her the truth, yet he couldn't lie to her. "Not really," he admitted. "The lack of laughter isn't something I'm used to. It's far too serious for my liking. And the wallpaper in my room is enough to drive a man insane."

Mia stopped walking to face him. She'd stood in the doorway of his room a few times. "It is pretty awful in there. All I can think is 'Redrum' every time I see it."

He chuckled as some of the tension eased from him. "If I turn into Jack Torrance from *The Shining* and start wielding an ax, you'll know why."

Mia laughed. "I can't see you as a psycho."

His eyes twinkled in the rays of the sun filtering over him. Those rays caressed his body in a way that emphasized his broad shoulders and gentle smile. There was something so open and honest about his smile and demeanor. Unlike others she'd encountered during her time running around the streets, and then in captivity, nothing sinister lurked beneath David's surface. With him, what she saw was what she got, and she wanted more of it.

Before she could think about her intentions, she pulled off a mitten and stretched up to brush back a strand of blond hair falling to the corner of his eye. He didn't move to touch her when her fingers stroked across his temple and down the angles of his cheekbone.

His skin was smooth, a strong contrast to the stubble she came into contact with next. The coarse hairs along his jaw prickled against her fingers as she ran them over his jaw and around to his chin. The predatory way he watched her made her pulse pick up. Her increasing breaths caused a steady plume of steam to form in the chilly air as she dared to dip her fingers toward his neck.

David watched the fascination playing over Mia's face as she continued to explore him. He'd been touched by many women over the years, but none of them had ever stroked him with such reverence. He wanted more of it, more of *her*.

His fangs lengthened when his eyes latched onto the pulse beating within her neck. After what she'd been through, she might never allow another to feed from her again, but he desperately longed to taste her.

The muscles in his forearms flexed when her fingertips rested against the vein in his throat. The heightened scent of her arousal caused his cock to harden in response. He gritted his teeth against the growing pressure of his erection. If she let him touch her, he'd have her stripped and be inside of her between this heartbeat and the next.

With a restraint he'd never known he possessed, he remained unmoving while she continued her exploration of him. The only way anything between them would progress was if she trusted him, and that would require patience.

She ran her fingers over his mouth. Her eyes dilated when she saw the tips of his fangs, and she licked her lips. Her dampened lips caused something within him to unravel. He lifted his hand to rest it over hers.

The gentle touch didn't cause the panic to immediately well within her, but Mia didn't know if it would soon. Sometimes, just when she thought she was perfectly fine, the panic would hit her out of nowhere, and she didn't want to take the chance of that happening right then. She was enjoying herself too much to risk ruining it by having a meltdown.

"Please just let *me* touch *you*," she whispered.

He suppressed a groan as his hand fell back to his side. He didn't know what he'd done to deserve such exquisite torture, but he knew he'd never deny her anything she asked of him. Mia's fingers dipped to the hollow of his throat. She ran them along the edge of his coat collar.

"Unzip it," he said hoarsely.

Mia's eyes flew up to his when he uttered the gruff command. "It's cold out," she protested.

"I'm anything but cold right now, Mia," he replied.

She swayed instinctively toward him as liquid heat spread between her legs. Like him, she was anything but cold. Her hands trembled as she pulled off her other mitten and shoved them both into her pockets. Taking hold of the coat's zipper she tugged it. When it was halfway down, she spread the heavy material wider and slipped her hands inside. She rested her hands on his chest, savoring the heat of his body as his skin rippled beneath her palms. The rigid muscle of his pectorals flexed when she moved her fingers over them. His heart beat so wildly she could feel every pulse of it against his ribs as if it were her own.

She inhaled the increasing scent of him as she slid lower over his chest toward his stomach. Her movements pushed the zipper farther down until her hands rested against the hard ridges of his abs beneath his navy blue sweater.

She'd never felt this attuned to anyone before, never been so aware of another's reaction to her as his muscles and skin rippled in reaction to her touch. Images of running her tongue over the entire length of him, of tasting every inch of his hard body, flashed through her mind until her knees went weak.

"You feel… amazing," she breathed.

"Do whatever you wish to me. I won't touch you until you tell me to," he promised. The way she pulled her plump lower lip between her teeth and nibbled on it had his cock hardening to the point of pain. He deserved to be named a saint after this, but he wouldn't touch her, not until she gave him the okay to do so.

"Anything?" she asked as her eyes flew up to his.

"Anything."

Her fingers slid lower to tug at the edge of his sweater. She pulled it up a few inches to reveal his tanned skin beneath. Between his woodsy scent, golden skin, and athletic body, David seemed to be made of the outdoors.

Before she could think, she flattened her palms against him and whimpered at the exquisite feel of his smooth skin stretched taut over his etched muscles. She traced every line of his abdomen before running her fingers down the trail of blond hair from his belly button to the waistline of his jeans. She drank in the evidence of his need for her in the heavy bulge outlined against his jeans.

The wetness between her legs grew as she imagined taking him deep within her and riding him until both of them were too exhausted to move. But that would mean being close to someone in a way she'd never been close with anyone before. She'd been with multiple men over the years, but she'd never been *close* with any of her partners. She didn't even remember their names; they had simply been a diversion.

She would be close with David though. She would be opening herself up to him in ways that mattered far more to her than sex did. Was she ready for that? No, she wasn't, or at least she didn't think she was. However, she'd long ago started living in the *now*. The past was too painful to stay in, the future too uncertain.

She may not be ready for what might develop with David, but right then she wanted to feel more of him, to explore him further.

Standing in the snow, at the edge of a lake, was not the way to do that.

"I think we should go back to the compound," she said.

David's breath exploded from him in a plume that danced in the air. *Patience*, he reminded himself. He'd never been an impatient man; he'd never seen the point of it. Things would happen as they did and in their time. Trying to rush them wouldn't make it happen any faster.

But his instincts were screaming at him to take her, to brand her, to make her *his*. He couldn't do any of those things, yet, but he'd been enjoying watching her explore him. He wasn't ready to have that stop.

"Then we will go," he somehow managed to get out.

Mia slid her hands away from his stomach, dipping them lower to his jeans where she cupped his heavy balls and throbbing erection. His lips skimmed back to reveal his lengthy fangs. She made a mewling noise the likes of which she'd never heard from herself before, as those fangs caused the yearning in her to grow deeper.

She'd been abused by those vampires who had placed her in chains. They'd hurt her in ways she'd never known possible when they'd drained her blood unwillingly from her, but she knew it wasn't always excruciating when vampires exchanged blood. And right now she craved David's bite almost as much as she craved his body.

"We are not done," she murmured.

David thought his heart was going to tear out of his chest when she said those words, and her hand stroked the rigid length of him through his jeans. If she would have allowed it, he would have scooped her up in his arms and run all the way back to the mansion with her. Instead, he watched as she stepped back and turned away from him.

CHAPTER SEVEN

MIA HAD BEEN with nearly two dozen men after her parents died, and had sex countless times, but the consuming *need* she felt for David was something new to her. With those other men, she'd been seeking comfort. She'd been looking to ease her curiosity about sex and a man's body. Looking to be in the now and to be close to someone again no matter how briefly.

Human or vampire, it hadn't mattered which she took into her bed, as long as she found them attractive and she could bury her sadness in sex for a bit.

Her first time with a man had been a month after the fire. At the time, she knew his name, but she only remembered him as number one now. She'd been able to forget her heartache for a bit in him, but she'd felt lost and alone again when they were done. However, those moments of experiencing flesh against flesh and having someone hold her in their arms had been a brief reprieve from her life. Those moments of being able to forget, no matter how small they were, had been addicting.

Before the fire, she would have waited forever until her mate came along before having sex. After, she hadn't believed in anything enough to continue to believe she would find her mate.

Though, at one time she'd truly believed that she'd felt her mate out there, somewhere. Or at least she thought she'd felt him waiting for her, back in the days when she'd been a teenager concocting silly fantasies of perfect worlds and perfect happiness.

Mia realized now that dreams of perfection were absurd, but she may have been right about one thing—her mate really might have been out there waiting for her already.

If David truly was her mate, and she was beginning to believe he was, why couldn't she have found him sooner? When she'd been so lost and alone after the fire? When no one had cared if she lived or died, not even her on some days?

The loneliness and misery following the deaths of her parents had been an unending gulf of despair that had threatened to ruin her, and it nearly had. She could have used someone to lean on then, to hold her and care for her, to let her know she was still loved when she'd never felt more unloved in her life.

But who would she be now, if she had lost herself in another that way, even if that other was her mate?

Her childhood had been sheltered and she'd known nothing but love. She'd never had to stand on her own. She would do anything to go back and change the night of the fire, to save her parents, but though there were times she'd hated herself over the years, hated her life and the things she'd done to survive, she was also proud of the fact that she was still here. That somehow she, a cloistered child who had never known hardship, had managed to survive things that would have broken others completely.

Sure, she had some serious issues that frustrated her to no end, and she'd made numerous mistakes, had things she would change in her life, but she was still *here*. She would survive this and get through it the best she could, just as she had everything else.

The first four years after the fire had been grueling, but one day when she was twenty-two, she'd sat herself down and taken a good look at her life. The newest vampire she'd been seeking comfort from had walked out her door without so much as a backward glance.

They'd been spending time together for nearly three months; nothing serious, no promises exchanged. If she really tried, she could probably remember his name, but from the very beginning she hadn't cared what it was and only thought of him as number twenty-three. She'd only cared about those minutes that she could experience with him which would allow her to keep from thinking.

When twenty-three left, she realized she'd spent three months with him, the longest she'd spent with anyone since her parents died, and she felt nothing about his departure from her life. He'd been just another man passing through, and not *one* of them had done anything to ease the sadness in her.

After her parents' deaths, she'd tried to bury her grief in one guy or another, and in one place or another, as she'd also moved constantly. In those four years, all she'd succeeded in doing was burying herself in an attempt not to think about what she'd lost, or grieve for it.

At one time, she'd dreamt of a family all her own. She used to love to read and learn, especially anything having to do with astronomy. The stars had always held a special place in her heart and fascinated her from the time she was old enough to look at them. After number twenty-three, she realized she hadn't read a book or stared more than passingly at the stars in four years.

She could blame her disconnect from life, and the things she'd once cared about, on the fact that everything had been torn away from her in a single night, but she knew it couldn't all rest there. She'd made her choices. She'd lain in those men's beds and tried to forget everything she'd once been in a cowardly endeavor to hide from the painful truth of being an orphan instead of facing it.

Maybe if she'd cared for any of those men she would have felt differently, but she hadn't given a crap about any of them. She'd used them far more than they ever could have used her.

On that day three years back, she'd realized she had nothing except endless loneliness and sadness ahead of her, unless she did something to change her life.

And change it she would. She became determined to get her life together. She knew it wouldn't happen all at once, but gradually she'd rebuilt it. She'd stayed off the dating scene, though she hadn't actually been dating any of those men, not really. She'd gone to the library and picked up books on astronomy once more.

She'd moved back to the East Coast from California. If she was going to rebuild her life, she couldn't continue to run and hide; she had to go home and face it. She'd never been able to bring herself to go back to what remained of the home she'd shared with her parents, but she'd at least made it back to Connecticut. It had been a huge step for her on her road to healing.

She'd enrolled herself in a couple night classes. She didn't know what she would ever do with an education, but school had been something to do with her time, and it had given her a purpose. She'd found a job at a local coffee shop and rented an apartment down the road from it.

She could have survived without a job; she'd fully matured by that point and could use her abilities with far more consistency. However, she'd spent the last four years taking from others and manipulating minds the best she could. She was determined to change that, to do something different with her life. To stand on her own.

On her days off work, she spent a lot of time exploring museums and traveling the coast to see the sights. She watched the sunset and stars appear from numerous locations. If she had any extra money, she put some in savings and donated the rest to a shelter in the city that specialized in runaway children. Twice a month she made the hour drive into Hartford to volunteer there.

Over the course of the next year, she was able to get the panic attacks plaguing her since the fire under control. She took back her life, and she finally *grieved*. For the first time since her parents died, she sat down and truly acknowledged everything that had been taken from her, and she wept.

She'd cried when they died, but only on that first night while she watched the flames consume everything she loved. She hadn't cried again until years later, and then she hadn't stopped for weeks on end, until one day she finally felt a scab healing over a wound she hadn't realized festered so badly.

For three years, she worked to rebuild herself. She abstained from sex, and she regained control of her life. Until three months ago, when all control had been torn away from her again....

Mia closed the door to her room, pulling the too-large coat off as she struggled against the memories trying to burst free. She draped the coat over the desk chair nearby and leaned against the door. David stood before her, his coat still unzipped, his body coiled as if he were about to pounce. She desperately wanted him, but if he touched her she may lose it and rethink everything about this.

How could she yearn for him so badly, yet still feel a burgeoning panic at the idea of him touching her?

Would she ever be normal again?

Mia shook her head and dropped it into her hands as she struggled to suppress the emotions and memories rocking her.

David took a step toward her before he stopped himself from getting any closer. Touching her would send her over the edge, but the battle he saw her waging with herself tore at his insides. He'd never felt so helpless in his life. He had no idea how to comfort the only woman he'd ever longed to comfort in his life.

"Mia—"

"I can touch you!" she cried, not sure if she was convincing him or herself of this. "Just let me touch you."

"If you're not ready for this, then let's go to the gym or swimming or something else. I'm not willing to risk pushing you away."

Tears pricked at her eyes, but she swiftly wiped them away. "I'm not sure I am ready for this," she admitted, "but I want you, and I want to try."

She didn't know what this would all mean. She may not be able to do more than touch him. Then again, she might be able to do much more, and she might end up discovering he wasn't her mate, but just another guy.

No, not just another guy. He would forever be David to her. He would never be number twenty-four. Already he meant more to her than any of the other numbers in her life.

David's eyes were drawn to the rise and fall of her breasts against the black sweater she wore. Despite her distress, the musky scent of her desire filled the air. He could ease her need—she might even let him if he went slow enough—but what would the consequences of that be? He'd seen Liam lose control. That loss of control was something he never would have believed his friend, or himself, capable of. He knew it could happen, and it could happen to him.

"If we do this, Mia, and you are my mate, it will advance things rapidly between us. The bond will have to be sealed. Before this progresses, you have to be certain you're ready for that."

"Do you always try to talk women out of touching you and possibly having sex with you?" she muttered.

"No, but I've never cared if they were still there the next day or not before. I do with you."

Mia sucked in a breath. "I've never cared if a man was there or not the next day either," she admitted. "Until now."

"If you're not ready now, I'll wait until you are," he told her.

"Why are you so understanding?" she whispered.

"Because you're worth it."

"You don't know that. You know so little about me."

"Then tell me about you. I want to hear it all."

"What about you and your life?"

"You know most of it already, or at least the important things about it, and you've met or at least heard of those I care for most. I'd prefer to hear about you right now, but I'll tell you anything else you want to know about me."

Mia stared at him before stepping away from the door, her gaze dropping to his erection. He had to be uncomfortable; there was no doubt what he would prefer to be doing with her right then, yet he was asking about her life. He may not be able to touch her, but they could both figure out a way around that. He wanted to know about *her*, and not as some attempt to get into her pants.

Her gut clenched. She knew there would be an intimacy between them she'd never experienced before if they did this. She had a feeling David could destroy her, if he walked out of her life or was taken from it. The funny thing was the thought didn't terrify her as she'd assumed it would.

"What do you want to know?" she asked.

"Tell me more about your life after your parents died. Tell me what you did and where you went after they were killed."

"As I said before, I went to Hartford first. We lived in a very rural area that was nothing like the city. I have no idea what drew me to the city, but it's where I found myself roaming around when I...." She paused as she tried to think of the right words to describe what it had been like for her. "Came to, I guess you could say. I spent those first couple days almost in a fugue state. When I became aware of my surroundings, I had no idea where I was. My feet were bare, black with dirt and soot and caked with both dried and fresh blood. I had no pants on, only the T-shirt I'd worn to bed the night of the fire, and it was a burnt, smoke-stained mess. My thighs had been burnt to the bone while I'd been trying to reach my parents during the fire, but they were already healing when I became aware of the burns again."

Her hands instinctively fell to rest over the burn scars still marring her thighs. "If they'd been normal injuries, they would have healed without any hint of damage left behind on me, but I still bear the scars. I think it's more than the burns being bone deep, or that I was an immature vampire at the time they occurred. I think it was also because my soul had been torn open too, and a part of me felt I deserved those scars for failing to save my parents when I succeeded in getting myself out."

David clasped his hands behind his back to keep from trying to console her when she lifted her head to look at him. In the powder blue of her eyes, he could almost see the flames of the fire playing through her memories. Her suffering washed off her in waves that he'd never felt from another before.

"The last memory I had before I came to in Hartford was standing in the snow, watching while the fire consumed my family. I could hear my mother's screams from within, but there was nothing I could do to get to her. I'd already tried and failed. Burns covered my face, my hands, my feet, but my palms and thighs were the worst."

"Why is that?" David inquired.

Mia turned her hands over to study her palms. Unlike her thighs, the skin on her hands remained clear of any blemishes. Her palms had been burned nearly as badly as her legs, but the burns hadn't covered as much of her body on her hands as they had on her thighs.

"When I first woke that night," she said. "I tried to get down the hall to my parents' room. Flames rolled across the ceiling over my head, but despite the glow of the fire, I couldn't see anything through the smoke."

That was an understatement. She'd never known darkness could be as complete as what she'd experienced in that hallway. The smoke clogging her nostrils, choking her lungs, and blinding her was something she would never forget. Nor would she forget the racing of her heart or the sweat streaking down her face and stinging her eyes.

"I swung my hands helplessly back and forth to feel my way along a hall I'd known inside and out only hours before. I remember feeling as if someone had dumped me into the middle of a fucked-up funhouse and twisted things all around on me, making it impossible to find my way to the one destination I never reached—my parents."

Mia kept her gaze on her palms as she continued to speak. "I was almost to their bedroom when the floor gave out beneath me."

She wiped away the sweat beading across her forehead as the memories she'd labored to overcome brought forth a wave of fresh panic. She'd gotten better at dealing with her grief, but she'd never revealed what had happened that night to anyone before. It made her feel almost as vulnerable as she'd felt in the fire. She had to get through this, had to finally face it completely, and David had to know just how deeply scarred she was both outside and in.

Lifting her head, she focused on him again. She may have stopped talking if she discovered pity in his eyes. Instead, she saw only compassion. "I plummeted into the living room. Before I could register my broken ankle, a burning beam fell across my legs, pinning me to the ground. The pain…."

Her screams echoed in her ears, and the blistering heat of the fire beat against her flesh once more. Sweat slid down her nape, gluing her sweater uncomfortably to her flesh. She didn't bother to pull it away. It had taken her years to realize there would never be any escaping her memories.

"At first the pain was so encompassing I couldn't move. All I could do was scream as the flames ate away at my skin and muscle. Then I heard my mother shouting my name and my survival instinct kicked in, as did my need to get to her. The beam was the size of a tree trunk, but terror gave me a rush of adrenaline. I shoved the beam off me enough that I was able to pull myself out from under it.

"I dragged myself toward the main foyer as debris and showers of sparks fell over me. The heat was impossible to escape as flames encompassed everything around me. I screamed for my mom the best I could through the smoke, but I'm not sure she ever heard me. When I got to the foyer, it was impossible to tell if the top half of the stairs still existed with all the smoke, but the fire had already consumed the bottom half."

Mia's gaze went beyond him to the window over his shoulder. The cardinal had returned to the tree. It ruffled its feathers and puffed itself out as it settled in, seeming to listen to her story too.

"I couldn't see my mom, but I could still hear her. I also knew I couldn't get to her, not that way, but there was no other way for me to go. My path to the back stairs was blocked by more fire."

CHAPTER EIGHT

MIA'S EYES deepened in color to an almost ocean blue as she spoke. With every word, her voice became increasingly raw and lanced with anguish. She sounded like smoke choked her once more, and David knew that in some ways it did—the memories, at least.

"What did you do?" he asked when she remained silent.

"I dragged myself to the front door. I pulled myself up to open it, before clawing my way across the porch, down the steps, and to the snow beyond. I can still recall the sound of my burnt flesh sizzling when it came into contact with the snow."

David winced and twisted his hands behind his back until he was sure he'd torn some of his skin away. It kept him from pulling her close though.

"Then I looked back and I knew it was over. There was no way I could get back inside to my parents. The fire was everywhere, and it consumed everything I'd ever known. I stood there until I heard the distant wail of sirens. I still had enough sense to know I couldn't be taken to a hospital. I think it was my last coherent thought."

"Until Hartford."

"Yes."

"What did you do there?"

"When I came back to myself, I managed to get a hotel room and clean myself up. I stole some clothes from the people in the room next to mine. Unable to stay there for long, I returned to the streets after I'd fed on those people. At the time, I couldn't pull myself together enough to do anything else. I had nowhere else to go, no one to turn to. As turned vamps, my parents' families had died years before. I'd been homeschooled, and I had no friends. My parents were all I'd ever known.

"So I wandered the streets, feeding from the people there and grouping together with other homeless teens. Our histories may have been different, but we all felt the cold and we were all doing everything we could to survive. I knew one day my abilities would grow enough that I wouldn't have to be homeless, yet I didn't care. There wasn't much I did care about during those days."

"That's understandable," David said when her gaze went to the window beyond him again.

"Eventually, I moved to Florida with some guy I met. I can't remember his name, only that he was number three, and the first vampire I was with."

David's teeth clamped together and his fangs lengthened at the mention of her and another man. He would have gladly torn the head from that man if he'd been standing in front of him right then. It was not a rational compulsion, but the idea of anyone else touching her made him feel anything but rational.

"Number three?" he grated out.

"I numbered the guys who moved through my life. It was easier that way, and I didn't really care to know their names."

"I see," he murmured.

Her eyes narrowed on him. "I'm not ashamed of my past or anything I've done in it. I may have some issues—okay, probably more issues than *Astronomy* magazine—but I'm a survivor. There are many who wouldn't have made it through what I have, and despite the fact I *hate* that there are times I can't control my own body, I am proud that I'm still here."

He could practically feel her anger blistering against his skin. No matter how jealous the knowledge of another man touching her made him, she was right. There were many who never would have made it out of that fire, never mind getting through everything that followed. She'd done what she needed to do to survive and stay anchored to this world. If she hadn't, he never would have found her.

Now that he *had* found her, he would do everything he could to keep her. If he became ensnared in his jealousy, he would ruin things with her. There may be an intricate bond between them, but they would have to work at trust and love. Being mated did not guarantee those things, and he wanted them both with her.

"You shouldn't be ashamed of anything that has made you who you are today, Mia," he replied. "I'm not even sure of the number of women I've been with, let alone remember all their names."

She'd kick him in the nuts if he ever judged her for the men she'd been with, but she had to admit the idea of other women out there, knowing what it was like to be with him, made her blood boil.

"I know the number," she said.

He nodded as he held his hands out before him in a conciliatory gesture. Her gaze fell to his reddened, chapped skin. The last of her annoyance melted away when she realized he'd done that to himself in order to keep from touching her. In that instant, she knew where the end of this conversation would lead them.

She lifted her gaze to his as she spoke her next words. "But there's only one who will matter."

Red flashed through his eyes, his nostrils flared as he inhaled sharply. He took a step toward her before clasping his hands behind his back and moving away once more. "Yes, there is."

The gravelly sound of his voice and the ravenous promise in his eyes sent a shiver of pleasure down her spine. Oh yes, he'd be completely different from all the others. She didn't care what she had to do; she *would* figure out a way to be with him. Today.

"What did you do after Florida?" he asked.

"From Florida I moved to Arizona, then New Orleans, Vegas, Dallas, Salt Lake City, and Santa Fe, before going on to Seattle, Portland, San Francisco, and finally L.A. I was in L.A. when I realized I'd been running for far too long and it was time to stop. I moved back to Connecticut and started piecing my life back together."

"How did you do that?" David inquired.

"One day at a time."

She stepped away from the door and walked around him toward the window. Unlike the hideousness of David's red room, her room was painted an off-white that emphasized the deep blue carpet and drapes surrounding the large picture window. Metal shutters were rigged to descend over the window at the press of a button, although she'd never hit that button as she much preferred to fall asleep to the stars and wake to the early morning sunlight.

Mia stopped before the window to gaze out at the snow before turning to perch on the edge of her bed. The thick mattress sank beneath her weight. She'd only spent a couple years living mainly on the street, but afterward she'd always been grateful for the softness of a mattress beneath her. While being held captive, a mattress had become a luxury she'd never believed she'd experience again.

Now it was a bit of heaven that never failed to make her sigh in contentment.

Mia gripped her knees when David settled onto the bed six inches away from her. She turned her head to him, her breath catching in her chest as his eyes sparkled in the rays of the sun streaming over him. Without thinking, she stretched her hand up to his cheek. He stiffened but made no move to touch her. Mia pulled her hand away.

"Sorry," she murmured.

"Don't *ever* apologize for touching me, Mia."

Her hands gripped her legs again.

"So, one day at a time," David prompted when it became apparent she wasn't going to speak again.

"I tried yoga, but it wasn't for me. Tried meditation too with no luck. From the time I was a little girl until the fire, I *loved* the stars. I'd often lie out at night staring at their changing patterns and dreaming of being amongst them. Many times my dad would join me and we would lie out beneath them together. He showed me the constellations and stars he knew. The ones he didn't, I would research and find out on my own. The planetarium was one of my favorite places to go, and I'd drag my parents there at least once a month. They loved me so much," she whispered.

He hated the sadness playing over her features at the mention of her parents. "Of course they did."

"So when I woke up and realized the life I'd been living for the past four years wasn't what my parents would want for me, I turned to the stars again to help get me through everything." She told him about her travels and how she would explore the stars at every new place she went to. Told him about her time volunteering at the shelter and the money she scraped together for the kids.

"My dream is to see the Aurora Borealis. I'd love to see the stars from space too one day, but I figure seeing the Northern Lights is a far more achievable goal right now," she said.

"I agree."

David watched the nuance of emotions playing over her face as she focused on the window again. She went from wistful to sad, then to excited and happy while she spoke. A small smile played at the corners of her lips.

"Maybe one day, if I live long enough, there will be a time when people go into space as easily as they fly across the country," she said. "I can hope so anyway. *Star Wars* was always my favorite movie. I'd *love* to be able to fly something like the *Millennium Falcon* through space."

He lifted an eyebrow at that. "Was Han Solo your first crush?"

"I was always more of a Chewie girl."

David's loud laugh caused her eyes to widen. She'd never heard anyone laugh like that, so deep and true. It was a laugh that would have made even a virgin drop her panties. It almost made her do so.

"Was it all of Chewie's hair that did it for you?" he asked between bouts of laughter.

Lured by his amusement, Mia edged closer until only an inch separated them. "The height," she murmured.

Her lack of a sex life for the past few years hadn't mattered to her. She'd thought little of it, as she'd been more focused on learning how to be happy with herself, but now it mattered. She instinctively knew David could satisfy her far more than any man, her own hand, or even her favorite vibrator ever had.

And she wanted him.

She inhaled the aroma of snow and pine adhering to him. Her fangs lengthened as her gaze fell to the vein in his throat. She'd fed from some of the humans she'd been with during sex—she had more needs than just sexual ones, after all—but she'd never fed from another vampire. She'd also never allowed herself to know what another was thinking or feeling while she fed, yet she found she *craved* that knowledge with him.

Her hand rested against his cheek, drawing his head toward her. His laughter faded away when his eyes met hers. Her gaze latched onto his full lips. Unable to resist the magnetic draw she felt to him, she moved forward to tenderly kiss him.

David's body reacted as if he'd been socked in the stomach. The air rushed out of him the second her lips caressed his. The warmth of her breath against his mouth was an intoxicating sensation that pulled him into its drugging depths. Her tongue flicked out to run over his lips. He knew he should pull away, stop her before it was too late, but he found himself lost to her while he waited to see what she would do next.

Her breasts were the merest brush against his chest when she leaned closer and slipped her tongue between his lips. David's hands fisted in the comforter to keep from dragging her against him.

Her tongue tangled with his as she lifted her hands to rest them against his chest. The minty taste of her mouth and her intrinsic rose scent flooded his senses. His dick ached with the need to be free, to be inside her. Like a snake charmer, she had him completely ensnared by the sensual spell she cast over him.

His fingers tore through the comforter when she nipped at his lip before drawing it into her mouth and sucking on it. Her fangs scraping his flesh was a tease that was almost too much for him to bear before her tongue slid over his once more. She'd be the death of him, and he'd open his arms and eagerly welcome it if she let him hold her.

Mia clasped his face with both of her hands as she rose to stand before him without breaking the kiss. Her heart hammered in her chest while anticipation raced through her. *Need.* It was all she could think when his tongue dipped into her mouth. Every thrust of his tongue became more demanding as it entwined with hers.

He remained rigid on the bed as her hands slid through his hair to clasp together against his neck. His legs opened to accommodate her when she took a step toward him. His knees brushed against her hips, the contact so minimal she barely felt it.

She'd never been kissed as if she were the only woman in the world, but that was how she felt when David kissed her. She would give anything to feel his arms closing around her, but she didn't dare initiate that much contact. He had her starving for more of him, but she had no way of knowing how her body would react to being locked down again.

Unclasping her hands, she slid them around to the open front of his coat, pushing it back from his shoulders and down his arms. The corded muscles beneath her hands flexed as he shrugged it the rest of the way off while still kissing her. Desperate to feel his flesh against hers, she clutched the bottom of his sweater and lifted it.

His mouth pulled away from hers when his arms rose to allow her to tug the sweater the rest of the way off. His electric blue eyes deepened to an almost midnight blue while he watched her.

"There will be no turning back," he said in a hoarse voice she barely recognized. His fangs flashed in the sun spilling over him as he spoke.

Mia didn't respond as she drank in the broad shoulders bared to her. He was the most magnificent man she'd ever seen. He had the body of a skier, long and solid with a supple grace. Her body clamored with the need to see and feel more of him. Her fingers skimmed over his right pec in little circles. Dipping lower, she traced the deep line that ran down the center of his abs toward that mouthwatering erection straining against his jeans.

Her body tingled in anticipation of taking it in her hand and stroking it until his back bowed and he demanded more. Through the denim fabric, she ran her finger around the head of his cock. She didn't care that there would be no turning back if they continued with this. All she wanted was him inside her. Screw the consequences.

His hips rose a little off the bed, seeking more of her touch. "I want you," she whispered.

She lifted her head to gaze at him. The muscles in his arms bulged, sweat beading on his forehead and slicking his chest muscles as his hands twisted deeper into her comforter. White stuffing poked through the deep blue from where he'd shredded the material.

"Mia—"

"Shh." She bent to run her tongue over his lips again. "No more talking."

Unable to stop himself, David released the comforter and wrapped his hand around the back of her head. She stiffened instantly, her breath rushing out of her in a hiss. Releasing her, he gripped the comforter again. Mia remained tensed against him, barely breathing as her lips skimmed his.

He inwardly cursed himself while he waited for her to pull away. Her head lifted, her eyes searching his as her fingers slid over his shoulders once more and a tremor ran through her.

"Let me do the touching," she whispered. "I know I can handle that."

He feared his teeth would break from the force with which he clamped them together, but he managed to get out a response. "I will."

It would be the toughest thing he'd ever done in his life, but he would do what she asked of him. Her tiny fingers stroked the head of his dick through his jeans once more. He'd never been so hard in his life; the pressure was becoming almost too much for him to bear. He sighed in relief when she found the button and slid it free before pulling down the zipper. His shaft sprang forward in anticipation of her touch.

She should have known he would go commando. Mia gazed down at the bead of moisture forming on the thick head of his cock. A driving need to taste him had her licking her lips in anticipation.

When she tugged at his waistband, David lifted his hips so she could pull his jeans over his knees and down to his shins. Kneeling before him, she unlaced his boots and tugged them off. They thudded on the carpet as she tossed them aside. She removed his socks before pulling his jeans the rest of the way off.

Resting her hands on his knees, her fingers moved over his thighs. Her hands were so nimble against his flesh that they barely touched him, yet her grazing caress had him on the verge of coming. Her fingers skimmed over his shaft before she bent forward to run her tongue over the head, licking away the bead of pre-cum there.

David tore deeper into the comforter, spilling more stuffing around him as he restrained himself from slipping his hand around the back of her head and clasping her to him. Her eyes lifted to him, a knowing smile curving her lips before she slid her mouth down his shaft, taking him deeper.

"Fuck!" he groaned as her hand and mouth worked him. And what a mouth it was. Deliciously hot and wet as she swirled her tongue over and around him, driving him closer and closer to the brink of release. Her eyes never left his as she worked him, the erotic sight of her nearly his undoing.

Mia had never known it was possible to be so aroused without ever being touched, but she'd never experienced anything as sexy as David with his legs spread around her and sweat glistening over his body. She moaned as her nipples hardened in response to his obvious arousal.

"If you don't stop, I'm going to come," he grated from between his teeth, his fangs barely visible behind his lips.

Mia's hand clasped more firmly around his thick shaft, letting him know that was what she wanted him to do. Never before had she brought a man to completion this way; she'd never wanted to, but she did now. Rising a little higher, she kept her eyes on his as she worked him faster, relishing in the salty taste of him and the silken skin stretched over his rigid length. She slid her tongue down the thick vein running through his cock, causing him to groan in response.

Her fingers didn't meet as she held him, and she couldn't take him all the way into her mouth, but it didn't seem to matter as his hips rose and fell in rhythm with her sucking. His head fell back, the muscles in his neck stood out as a shout vibrated his chest and the hot rush of his release filled her mouth.

Mia took all of him into her before running her tongue around him once more and reluctantly releasing him. White stuffing from the comforter fell around her and onto the floor when David's head tipped back down to look at her. The savagery on his face robbed her of her breath.

She'd believed he would be more relaxed after finding his release, but he appeared coiled tighter than he had been before. On his face and in his eyes, she saw the absolute truth.

There was no going back.

CHAPTER NINE

"Now you," David growled.

Mia struggled to breathe while he continued to watch her as a hunter watched its prey. The hunger on his face, a hunger so similar and yet so different than those of the vampires who had drank from her in the warehouse, should have frightened her. She knew he not only wanted her body, but also her blood. Instead, she found herself becoming more stimulated by the realization. All of her clothes felt too abrasive as they rubbed against her hypersensitive skin.

"Now me," she murmured.

"Let me see you. *All* of you."

A thrill went through her at his commanding tone. With any other man, she would have flipped him the bird for thinking he could order her around in such a way. She would have walked out the door. Now she found her hands going to the edge of her sweater and sliding it up to bare her midriff before exposing her bra.

David's hands jerked forward, rending the comforter further while he watched Mia's slow, provocative movements. He took in her pale skin, round hips, and ribcage before she uncovered the bottom of her bra. It was simple and white, yet he found that bra to be one of the most alluring things he'd ever seen.

Ruby-colored eyes met Mia's when she tossed her sweater onto the floor and rose to stand before him. She'd never felt more desired or powerful in her life as his rapt gaze watched while she glided her hands down her belly until she reached the button of her jeans. She undid it and slid them slowly down her legs. With her toes, she kicked aside her jeans to stand before him in nothing but her bra and panties.

David's gaze ran over her slender body, drinking in every inch of her. Still thin from her captivity, the outline of her ribs was barely visible beneath her ivory skin. The only marks on her were the darker patches of skin on her upper thighs. There, her skin was not a creamy porcelain, but puckered and a deep pink from the burns she'd sustained in the fire.

His hands jerked again, not because he wanted to grab her and drive himself into her but because he wanted to pull her close and hold her to him. To embrace her while he tried to shelter her from the horrors of her past. He could have lost her in that fire.

Mia held her breath as David stared at her scars. When she'd first been burned, she'd been ashamed of them. Ashamed that she'd failed her parents, that she'd survived when they hadn't. She'd found them revolting. Now they were a mark of everything she had survived. They were a mark of who she was.

Some men had been repulsed by her scars, others had barely noticed them in their rush to screw her, but none had ever asked about them. David didn't have to ask; he already knew. When he lifted his eyes to meet hers, she didn't know what to expect to see there, but it certainly wasn't the pride blazing from him. That pride caused a lump in her throat and made her long to please him even more.

"You're beautiful," he told her.

The truth she heard in those words left her speechless. She was a little too thin right now, but she was still aware that she was far from ugly. However, she'd never felt beautiful before. She did now.

A smile tugged at the corners of his lips before he leaned subtly forward. "Now off with the bra," he ordered.

Mia quirked an eyebrow at him, but she did as he asked and unhooked her bra before tossing it aside. His eyes latched onto her bared breasts and her enticing pale pink nipples. He'd give anything to be able to touch them, to draw one of those buds into his mouth and nip at it before swirling his tongue around it.

"What would you do if you were touching me?" she asked.

His eyes snapped up to hers, his erection surged back to life as his heart thudded in his chest. "If I tell you, will you do it?"

Mia swallowed heavily. "Yes," she croaked out.

David ran his tongue over his fangs when they throbbed almost as badly as his dick did. "I'd run my hands over your breasts," he told her. "Taking them within my palms as I fondled them."

His eyes latched onto her hands as they slid up her flat belly to cup her small breasts. He found it increasingly difficult to continue speaking, but he'd talk non-stop if it meant he could watch her touching herself in such a way.

"Then I'd run my thumb over your nipples, savoring the feel of them as the peaks hardened until you begged for my mouth on them."

Mia's breath came in heavy pants as she did what he described and ran her fingers over her nipples until they hardened. She'd pleasured herself countless times over the years, especially since she'd started abstaining. Just because she'd chosen to focus on *her* didn't mean she hadn't missed orgasms.

But this was so completely different than those times when she'd been with other men. Completely different than when the need of her body had become too much for her to take and she'd slid her hand between her legs to ease it.

This wasn't screwing or scratching an itch. This was something so much more. It wasn't his hands stroking her, yet the way he stared at her made her feel as if they were the ones sliding over her body now. The intensity of his stare already had her on the brink of orgasm. If he ever did touch her....

If she didn't shy or run away from him, she knew she'd come apart completely in his arms.

"Then I'd pinch your nipple. Harder." His lips skimmed back when Mia did what he commanded. She moaned at the sensation of her fingers pulling at her flesh. "While caressing your breasts, I'd run my tongue over those nipples to soothe them before pinching them again."

"What then?" she gasped as her body clamored for release.

"Then I'd run my hands down your sides toward your panties while my mouth continued to feast on your breasts." He watched her hands slide down her sides, her head falling back so her pert breasts jutted mouthwateringly toward him. "I'd follow my hands with my mouth, down to the edge of your panties, and I'd take them in my teeth."

Her fingers hooked into the band of her underwear. "Then?" she whispered, anticipation pulsing inside her.

"Then I'd pull them off you, taking my time to explore every inch of you with my hands and mouth as I went. Take them off, Mia, *slowly*."

This domineering side of him was something she hadn't known existed, but she reveled in it as she slid her underwear down her legs.

"Lie down on the bed," he ordered.

Mia stepped out of her underwear and strolled over to the bed, her hips swaying. She felt his gaze on her every step of the way as she climbed onto the bed, her ass in the air. The rending sound of fabric followed her.

Mia's heart leapt into her throat when she glanced over her shoulder to find his blood-red eyes watching her. For the first time since she'd started this, trepidation slithered through her. She burned for his touch, but if he grabbed her what would happen? Would she turn him away? If she refused him, would he forcefully take from her as those other vampires had?

Before this had started between them, her answer to that final question would have been a resounding *no*. David would never harm her. But she'd never seen anyone so close to the brink of losing all control as he was right then. His lips had compressed into a flat line, the veins in his arms standing starkly out as his muscles trembled with his restraint.

David lifted his eyes to hers when she hesitated and a wave of distress washed off her. He knew he had to look half wild, but when she'd crawled across the bed with her round ass in the air, he'd nearly pounced on her like a cat on a mouse.

"I won't touch you," he vowed. "I won't make you do anything you're not comfortable with."

"How… how do I know you'll be able to keep control of yourself?" she stammered.

His fingers dug into the comforter as his gaze lifted to the posts of the bed behind her head. "I promise I won't, but if it will make you feel better, you can tie my hands to the posts."

"You'll easily be able to break free of any ties."

"You'll be able to get away from me before I do."

The problem was she didn't know if she'd want to get away from him before he broke free, and if he grabbed her she may freak out. Or she could remain completely calm and not freak out at all. It wasn't a chance she was willing to take.

She knew she should put a stop to this, but she couldn't bring herself to move away from him. She wanted him, and it had been so long since she'd taken anything for herself.

"I promise, Mia, I won't hurt you. We can end this now. All you have to do is say 'stop.'"

She gazed uncertainly at him before climbing off the bed. David watched her walk away before releasing his death grip on the comforter. His knuckles ached when he opened them, flexing his fingers. He didn't know what she would choose until she came back to him with two pieces of white cloth in her hand. It took him a second to realize the two pieces were belts from the thick robes stashed within every bedroom of this place.

He was so hard he couldn't think straight as she neared to stand before him. David pulled his legs onto the bed and slid up to rest his back against the thick chestnut headboard.

Mia glanced between his wrists and the solid bedposts. They'd hold a human without a problem, but he could break them in a second. "Are you sure?" Mia asked, uncertain if she was talking to him or to herself.

"Am I sure I want to be tied up by you while you do whatever I command or whatever you wish to me? Oh, I'm fucking positive, Mia."

Her body quickened with fresh yearning at his words. *No going back.*

He was magnificent and he could be hers, if she would allow it. But did she dare? Sex with someone was one thing, but letting someone in was a whole other thing completely. It may already be too late for that, she realized. She'd already opened herself up and revealed far more of her life to him than any of the other men she'd been with over the years.

But she was petrified of what lay ahead. All of the other life-changing events she'd gone through had been bad—really bad. And this *would* be life-changing; she didn't try to lie to herself and say it wouldn't. However, she couldn't see anything with David being bad. It simply couldn't be, not when he made her feel so alive and powerful.

She gazed at his hands as he held them out to her. Taking a deep breath, she decided to continue living in the now. She stepped closer to him and tied one of the belts around his right wrist before looping it around the pole.

"I've never…." She glanced at him from under lowered lashes.

"I'm happy to be your first, then." The predatory smile he gave her had her hurrying to finish what she'd started.

Her heart hammered as she climbed back onto the bed and eased herself carefully over his long legs as he spread them out in front of him. His eyes tracked her every move when she took hold of his left wrist. Her fingers caressed the pulse pounding in his wrist before she looped the terrycloth around it and pulled his hand toward the other post, wrapping the belt around the post and cinching it. With nothing left to do, her gaze nervously went back to his. Her nipples puckered when she discovered his eyes on her breasts.

She sat over him, her knees straddling his legs as she tried to figure out what to do. His erection jutted enticingly up between them, the head of it glistening with pre-cum once more. Just looking at it made her throb with need. He'd let her do whatever she wanted to him, yet the strength of the powerful muscles beneath her made it clear he was anything but helpless.

Reaching out, she hesitatingly trailed her fingers down his chest. His muscles rippled beneath her touch as his hands gripped the belts and pulled them taut. The wooden posts creaked from the force he applied to them, but he didn't pull on them again. His skin was supple beneath her hand, though it covered muscle that felt like steel. Crisp blond hair sprinkled his chest and encircled the nipples she rolled between her fingers.

"It's your turn to be satisfied, Mia," he said in a hoarse voice.

Her head tilted to the side as she watched him. Her fingers lifted to trace the curve of his full lower lip. "What would you do to me next?"

His eyes filled with red again when they came back to her. He blinked as he seemed to try to recall where they'd been. For a second, the electric blue of his eyes slid forth to mix with the red. His eyes latched onto the dark brown curls between her thighs, shielding her from his view. Kneeling before him, her breasts heaved with her shallow breaths. She may shy away from his holding her, but her body was begging for him.

"You're aching for release right now," he said.

Her eyes came up to his and for the first time red color crept across her cheeks. He didn't think it was from embarrassment, but the needs of her body. "Yes," she murmured.

"I'd give that to you, Mia, by running my hands over your thighs. Then I'd follow them leisurely with my tongue as I tasted every inch of you."

She whimpered and her hands fell to her thighs. "Then what?"

"Then I would dip my fingers inside you, stroking you in and out with one finger and rubbing against your clit until you were writhing beneath me. Touch yourself, Mia, but as your fingers slide into you, picture mine rubbing against you, fucking you deeper and deeper until you're on the verge of coming."

His heart raced as he watched her fingers sliding through her curls. She gasped, her body arching toward him as she dipped a finger into herself. "Are you picturing me?" he demanded.

"Yes," she moaned.

David bit his lip, drawing blood, but he barely noticed it as he watched her in fascination. "When you were begging for more, I'd stretch you farther by slipping two fingers inside of you to better prepare you for me, but I wouldn't enter you. Not until I was sure you could take me."

"What if I was already ready for you?"

David's hands tightened on the cloth bindings, stretching the fabric taut. "Then I'd slide my fingers away from you and draw you against me." Mia's hand fell away and she crept closer to his waist as he spoke. "Taking hold of my cock, I'd guide it into you until I buried myself all the way inside you."

Her hips moving against him caused him to buck at the sensation of her wet warmth sliding over his dick. Her palms pressed flat against the headboard as she bent until her lips barely touched against his. David remained immobile, letting her feel her way along until her tongue slid over his lips and she licked away the blood that had trickled down his chin.

He opened his mouth to her questing tongue and the sweet taste of her filled his senses. His tongue entangled with hers when her hands clasped his cheeks while she deepened the kiss. She moved her hips over him once more until she was in a position to take him into her body.

The warm heat of her sheath gripped the head of his cock as her body parted to allow him to partially enter her. The creaking of the wood forced him to ease his grip on the ties as she parted farther to his invasion, and his dick was gripped by her tight muscles.

"Mia," he groaned against her mouth when she froze above him, and her kiss stilled.

Her fingers trailed across his cheeks, her breath warming his mouth while her lips brushed his. He was caught in a tumultuous hell of sensation and need as he remained only partially buried within her. He could tear the binds free, grab her hips, and drive himself into her before she could get away from him. He could ease the strain in his body and take his release, but he would lose her if he did.

Deep breaths. He didn't dare move for fear he would do exactly that to her.

She pulled back to stare at him. He couldn't tear his gaze away from the vulnerability he saw in her beautiful blue eyes. He forgot all about his compulsion to bury himself within her and give them the release he knew they both needed. Right then, it was only the two of them in this moment—a moment unlike anything he'd ever shared with another.

Then her tight muscles eased around him and she slid down to take him fully into her. His hands instinctively jerked against the binds as her body gloved his cock perfectly. The overwhelming sensation of being buried within her nearly caused him to come before she even moved. He gritted his teeth against the impulse as she remained immobile on top of him, her eyes searching his.

It had been years since she'd had sex. She wasn't used to having another within her, but Mia nearly cried at the feeling of completeness that came with David stretching and filling her. She couldn't stop staring at him as a muscle in his jaw ticked to life while red and blue flashed through his eyes.

He looked so volatile and feral, yet he didn't try to tear free of his bonds. He didn't move beneath her, allowing her to adjust to his size and waiting to see what she would do. His barely restrained control was evident in the harsh lines of his face, yet he put her needs ahead of his, something no one had done for her since her parents died.

She bent to kiss his chin. He tensed when her nipples came into contact with his chest, and she lifted her hips so he slid a little out of her before she lowered herself down again. She moaned as the rigid length of him completely filled her once more.

Leaning back, she gazed down at him. A thin layer of sweat glistened across his body. All his muscles stood out starkly, and a vein pulsed in his forehead. She'd never seen anyone so magnificent. He deserved better than her and all of her many inadequacies, but he was hers and she was never going to let him go.

The exquisite friction of him sliding in and out of her as she began to move faster became all she could think about. Her fingers trailed down his chest as she traced over his muscles there, learning every dip and hollow, how he reacted to her touch, and what pleased him. With other men she hadn't bothered to learn what they enjoyed, she'd simply wanted to ease her need, but she couldn't get enough of exploring David and studying his reactions to her.

When she looked at him again, his eyes were latched onto her breasts as they moved and swayed before him. She took hold of them and circled her thumbs over her nipples. His lips skimmed back to reveal his fangs, but he didn't try to strike and sink them into her. She pinched her nipples as he'd asked her to do earlier, and his hips rose off the bed. She gasped when the movement drove him deeper into her.

Resting her hands on his shoulders, she pushed back on him, grinding her hips against his. His heels dug into the bed to lift his hips again. He thrust hard into her, and she cried out in ecstasy. A coiling tension built within her, spiraling higher and higher as he plunged deeper and deeper until it felt as if he touched a piece of her soul.

Screwing had always been pleasurable enough before, but it had never been anything like this. She *had* to connect with David, to have him within her, possessing her. And she wanted more. Her eyes fell to the vein in his throat, pulsing with every rapid beat of his heart. Her fangs lengthened, saliva filling her mouth as thirst seared her veins.

"Do it, Mia."

As before, she was helpless to disobey his commands. With lightning speed, she sank her fangs deep into his vein. The hot wash of his blood slid down her throat, and she mewled as joy scorched her. Her hands resting against his chest kept her from pressing her body fully against his—she still didn't trust herself to have so much skin contact with him—but the heat of him warmed her skin as his blood filled her in ways she'd never been filled before.

Her body rose and fell faster as his mind opened to hers, and his undeniable bliss engulfed her. The overwhelming sensations caused her head to spin and her body to ache in the most wondrous of ways.

David's body arched beneath hers as she drained his blood in greedy pulls, and her body rocked against his. His arms jerked involuntarily against the binds. The wooden beams cracked as the cotton fabric shredded and fell around him. He managed to keep himself from seizing her waist by slamming his hands onto the headboard. The wood splintered beneath his palms while he held onto it. Her movements became more demanding as he felt her nearing the brink.

She retracted her fangs from his neck and rose to ride him faster. He hungrily drank in the wanton way her body moved over his as her hands ran over her breasts, cupping them and rolling them within her palms. Her head fell back and she cried out as her muscles gripped his shaft.

The force of her climax was his undoing. He drove his heels into the bed as he buried himself deeper into her and found his release as her body hungrily pulled his semen from him. More wood splintered beneath his hands, but he managed to maintain his hold on the bed as her muscles continued to contract around his cock.

Delicious shivers rolled through Mia as she slumped against his chest. She'd just experienced the most mind-blowing orgasm of her life.

Most times, she'd found a form of distraction in sex. A few times she'd stared at the ceiling and pondered what to do for the rest of the day, but what had just transpired between her and David had been beyond simple sex.

What they'd shared was something far deeper and more intimate than anything she'd ever known before. Something within her had shifted and changed when they'd joined together. Something was still shifting and changing as his blood flowed within her. She already wanted more of him, more of his taste and feel, more of *everything*.

Even now, her body continued to grip at his shaft while she felt the ongoing pulse of his release deep within her. His blood blending with hers warmed her almost as much as his body did. She nestled against him, inhaling his woodsy scent and the scent of their joining as it mingled in the air.

Protected, safe, cherished. For the first time since her parents died, that was exactly how she felt. She'd come home in his arms. She'd been so lost, but now she'd found exactly where she was always supposed to be. Tears pricked her eyes. His lips nuzzled the top of her head as her fingers dug into his solid chest.

The heat of him, the feel of his skin against hers, wrapped her within a warm cocoon, trapping her there. Her chest constricted and her breath hitched as her haze of euphoria slipped away. The sensation of skin against skin woke something more in her, something she'd somehow managed to bury for a bit.

His woodsy scent faded away as her memories thrust her back to another time and another place. The vile aromas of body odor, fear, blood, and death encompassed her as she found herself chained to a wall once more. The bed was no longer beneath her. Instead, she felt the cold of the concrete floor she'd slept on for an unknown period of time before they'd moved her to the warehouse.

Her bones dug into that floor. No matter how she moved, she couldn't escape the cold permeating her flesh. She didn't cry; she was too tired and too weak for tears as the vampires drained her of her blood over and over again. Their hands were on her, their laughter in her ears….

She shoved herself away, reeling as the memories threatened to bury her.

CHAPTER TEN

DAVID SLIPPED out of her as she swung her leg away from him and scooted to the other side of the bed. Closing her eyes, she battled against the waves of panic threatening to choke her as her breath came in rattling hitches.

One, two, three, four, open your eyes and look at the floor.

Her gaze focused on the rug, on their clothes lying scattered across it as she tried to bury the laughter and cold once more. She clasped her head in her hands and focused on her bra as her body instinctively rocked forward and back.

"Easy, Mia," David said. He didn't dare release his hold on the headboard to comfort her. "I'm not going to touch you."

Mia inhaled a ragged breath and nearly choked on the lump of tears clogging her throat. What they'd just shared had been beyond anything she'd ever experienced before in her life, and now she was a freaking mess all over again.

"What is *wrong* with me?" she cried. "Why are you so understanding when I'm so broken?"

Her shoulders heaved as she turned tear-filled eyes to him.

David's fingers dug into the wood at the shattered look on her face. "You're not broken," he assured her.

"Fractured, then?" she demanded, recalling what he'd said to her before. "I'd say I'm a whole lot more than fractured when I can screw you but I can't let you hold me, or let myself touch you for too long without feeling as if I'm going to suffocate on my memories."

David sighed and released the headboard, holding his hands up when she edged farther away from him. Flexing his knuckles to get some blood flowing back into them, he lowered his hands to the bed. He understood her frustration; he felt it too, as he wanted nothing more than to cradle her close.

"We didn't *screw*," he said and her eyebrows went up. "You know what just happened between us was different from any other experience you've ever had with a man. It was definitely far different from any of my experiences with other women."

Being with her had altered something within him. No matter what, he knew she would be his from here on out. The good, the bad, and the ugly—whatever life threw at them, they would be together, and he would do everything he could to keep her protected. He may not be able to hold her, yet, but there would never be another for either of them again.

Mia's shoulders hunched forward. She drew her bottom lip into her mouth as she recalled everything that had transpired between them. The sensation of being home had been so welcome and wonderful. The way he made her body come alive made her long to have him inside of her once more.

"It was definitely different," she admitted. "Far different, but can't you see that only makes it worse? For a time, I felt different while I was with you. I felt powerful and in control again." He'd given her that control, and she'd given him another meltdown afterward. "I felt as if I finally belonged, yet I'm still… I'm still… *this*!" she cried and ran a hand down the front of her body. She tried to fight it, but tremors shook her hand. "I'm still a fucking disaster!"

"You're being too hard on yourself again. The things you have endured will take time to get over," he told her. "But look at how far you've already come. I bet when you woke up this morning, you never thought you'd be having the best sex of your life before nightfall."

Mia's mouth fell open and, despite her disgust with herself, a short burst of laughter escaped her. The playful look on his face relaxed her shoulders. She found herself easing back on the bed to sit so that she could feel the heat of his thigh against her. "Who says it was the best sex of my life?"

"Like you can honestly claim it wasn't," he replied, his blue eyes twinkling with amusement as a smile curved his mouth.

"If it was the best sex of my life, it was definitely the best sex of yours."

"You'll never hear me deny it." He folded his hands in his lap. "And it will only get better from here on out."

"Who said I was going to have sex with you again?" she teased.

His smile revealed all his perfect white teeth and the points of his fangs. "I can smell that you already want me again. Besides, there's no way you're not curious about all the things I'll be able to do to you without my hands."

Her heart thudded against her ribs, her nipples hardening at his words. David's smile slid away and he gripped the headboard again as a feral gleam shone in his eyes. His softening cock rose once more.

"I'll ease that curiosity for you," he promised.

Mia took a deep breath as a fresh wave of panic fell over her, but she still found herself unable to resist crawling toward him. His pull over her was greater than the moon's on the tides. His eyes never left hers as she straddled him once more.

"David?"

"Yes," he murmured as he ran his fingers over Mia's hair, the only part of her he could touch for any length of time without causing her to stiffen against him. Over time, she would get better at allowing him to touch her more and more; he had complete faith in that. She didn't see how much better she already was, how different she was from the skittish and beaten woman who had first stepped into this place. Some days she had setbacks, but almost every day was a new step forward for her. For *them.*

"I'd like to go with you to your home," she whispered.

David's fingers stilled as he lifted his head to prop it up on his hand. Mia continued to stare out the window while he gazed down at her. "If you don't think you're ready—"

"I am."

She rolled over to face him. He'd found a new comforter for them in a hall closet, a deep blue one that brought out the color of her eyes. The moon spilling across her bare breasts and dusky nipples created an inviting trail he longed to follow with his tongue. *One day.* And he would patiently wait for that day to come.

"I'd like to meet your family," she said.

"There are a lot of them," he warned.

"I know. I've heard the stories, but I *am* going to do this."

She gave a decisive nod as she said those last six words and her chin rose defiantly. He could sense her distress, but determination blazed in her eyes. He stroked her hair again and bent to tenderly kiss her lips. "Yes, you are," he whispered when he pulled away from her.

"And one of these days, I'm going to make you do all the work in bed."

Laughing loudly, he instinctively went to pull her into his arms, stopping himself in time. His arms dropped back to his sides, but she had caught the movement. Anger swirled in her eyes before they darted to the ceiling. That anger wasn't for him, he knew, but for herself. No matter what he said to her, she would continue to beat herself up for what she saw as a failure and a weakness on her part. One day, she would realize how strong she was.

"I look forward to it," he told her.

"I think…." Mia's voice broke as she grappled to get her words out. "I think you could drink from me too. My wrist, maybe. I think I can do that."

His nostrils flared and red swirled around his eyes as his need for her blood blasted against her. She didn't feel fear though, not like she'd felt when those other vampires had gazed at her before they'd taken her blood. David would be gentle. He wouldn't take more than he needed. He would see to her welfare above his own, and looking at him she realized how badly he needed to taste her. How badly he needed *her*.

"You have no idea how much I want to share blood with you, but I don't want you to *think* you can do it. I want you to *know*. I won't do anything to frighten you or risk pushing you away, Mia."

"But I can feel your thirst for my blood and I've been inside your mind. I know what you want from me."

"And I can control myself until you're ready."

"Even if we are mates? Will you be able to control it until I can be *sure* I can handle you feeding from me? What if that takes months?"

He opened his mouth to say he could control it for as long as necessary. Then he recalled Liam nearly losing his mind before completing the bond with Sera. That had been over thirty years ago now, but the memory had been etched into his mind, as had the knowledge of what could happen to a vampire when the mating bond was incomplete.

"Do you doubt we are mates?" he asked, because he certainly didn't, not after what had transpired between them. Not with the possessive way he felt about her. He already wanted her again, and he knew he'd never get enough of being with her.

Mia placed her hand over where his heart beat so solidly in his chest. "I think it's all moving very fast, but I can't deny I've never felt like this about someone before. I desire you in a way I've never desired another, but this is more than attraction between us. This is more like…."

"Like what?" he prodded when her voice trailed off.

"Like I belong." Her sweeping black lashes fell to cover her eyes before she lifted them to look at him once more. "With you."

"You do belong with me."

The absolute assuredness of his voice lured her closer until she could feel the heat of him against her skin, but they didn't touch. "Then you should feed from me too. If we're mates, it will make you unsettled if the bond isn't completed between us. I'll feed from you again while you're doing it."

David wanted nothing more than to sink his fangs into her, to taste her blood and bind them for eternity. To know what it was like to be a part of her in *every* way. He found himself lured toward her as his eyes latched onto the vein throbbing in her neck. Briskly shaking his head, he pulled away from her as he tried to rid himself of the drive to feed from her.

"Not until you're ready to be bound to me." He had no idea where he garnered the strength to utter those words. "Not until you're sure you *are* my mate and you're sure I can drink from you without overwhelming you. You'll have no doubts when the bond between us is completed."

"Are *you* so sure we're mates?"

"Yes."

His blunt answer startled her. She fumbled for a reply, then found herself simply saying, "Well then."

"And one day you will be too."

She loved his confidence, his arrogance. Any other man, she would have laughed in his face, but with David, she found it sexy as hell. She smiled at him and ran her fingers over the dark blond stubble lining his jaw.

"What makes you so sure?" she asked.

"Because you'll never be able to get enough of me. I know it. However, I'll gladly stay in this bed with you for as long as it takes to get you to agree with me."

She laughed as she leaned closer to him. "If that's the case, I may deny it for the rest of my days."

He smiled at her as he gripped the end of her hair and gave it a playful tug. "Don't tempt me, Mia."

She placed her head back on her pillow and gazed up at him. She couldn't deny that being mated to this man sounded completely appealing and *right*. She'd never get enough of the sensation of coming home when she was around him, and she had a feeling it would only increase over time.

But would she ever be able to give him everything he would need from her? Would she ever be what he deserved, someone who could love him openly and not be overwhelmed by fear when touched? There was only one way to find out, one step at a time. And she was determined to try.

"Tomorrow, we'll go to meet your family," she said.

"Mood killer," he muttered, and she giggled. "You better get some sleep, then. You're going to need plenty of rest to deal with that brood."

"I'm looking forward to it."

It astonished her to realize she actually was.

CHAPTER ELEVEN

David glanced over at Mia as she sat silently beside him while the highway passed by in a blur of signs and cars outside the windows of the Camry. Aiden had blindfolded them and taken them out of the compound early that morning, after they'd all said their good-byes to each other. Vicky and Abby had given him smug smiles and called him Shemp as they hugged him, but he couldn't deny he would miss them.

Aiden had driven them to the nearest car rental place and removed their blindfolds. "I'll be home for Christmas or at least Christmas Eve," Aiden told him.

"Your sisters?"

"I don't know. I know Abby plans to go home for Christmas Eve, but I'm not sure Vicky's ready yet. Abby won't leave her alone on Christmas if Vicky decides to stay behind."

"No, she won't," David agreed. "We'll see you soon."

He'd closed the door on Aiden and walked inside to rent a car. Mia hadn't spoken since they'd left New York behind, and they were nearly to the Maine border. A look of determination etched her features, but she had a white-knuckled grip on her legs as she stared out the window.

They still had over four hours to go before they arrived at his home near the border of Canada, along the coast of Maine. It was a beautiful place, one he couldn't wait to show her, but he would turn around if she asked him to. She had to be nervous about meeting everyone, and he couldn't blame her. He would be overwhelmed if the situation were reversed, but he knew she'd grow to love it there, and that she would be welcomed with open arms.

"You know," she said when they crossed into Maine, "you've asked a lot about me, and you know a lot, but you never asked me how I ended up in that warehouse."

David's hands clenched on the steering wheel, a sneer curving his lips as a snarl tore from him. Recalling her chained to the wall made his blood boil. The image of her with only her bra on and so many bites covering her that he couldn't see her skin through the dirt and markings was something he would never forget.

She'd been rank with terror and body odor, yet something about her had still captivated him when he'd first seen her. Even after they'd freed Vicky from the wall, he never would have left that building without Mia.

Quaking with the fury racking him, David switched through the lanes of traffic before pulling to a stop on the shoulder. His shoulders heaved as he tried to regain control of himself.

Mia leaned away from him, her back pressing against the door of the car as the waves of wrath emanating from him beat against her skin. He would never hurt her, she knew, but she'd never seen him like this. Controlled, teasing, self-assured—that was the David she knew. This David would slaughter anyone who made one wrong move toward either of them.

"David," she whispered.

"It's not that I didn't want to know how you got there," he bit out. "I didn't think you were ready to talk about it."

"I wasn't," she admitted.

Was she now? She had no idea, but she'd brought it up, and it had been for more of a reason than she was looking to pass the time with conversation. This wasn't exactly her ideal topic. She could have spent hours, days even, discussing the stars. Instead, she'd gone with the 'oh hey, you never asked how I came to be chained to a wall' topic of conversation. There had been a reason for it. She suspected it was because she needed to talk about it, and he was so easy to talk to.

Inhaling a shuddery breath, he lifted his head to look at her. His eyes were more vibrant than the purest of rubies. His fangs had sliced into his bottom lip, and two trickles of blood slid down his chin.

Despite his obvious rage, she leaned forward and licked away the beads of blood. She sighed when the potent taste of it hit her tongue. His body relaxed somewhat against her, and when she pulled back, his red eyes held a bluish tint to them.

"That's better," she murmured as she ran her hand over his bicep. "Would you like to talk about how you ended up there now?"

"I… I didn't think it would upset you so much."

Before she could blink, he captured her hand. Instinctively, she tried to jerk away from the abrupt movement and the pressure of his hand around hers. He held on for the briefest of seconds before releasing her. Shoulders hunching forward, he ran a hand through his disordered hair and stared at the steering wheel.

She'd heard vampires could become unstable if they discovered their mate and the mating bond wasn't completed, but if they were mates, they were in the beginning stages of it. She'd never seen him like this though and she suspected there was more to his apparent instability than her mentioning her imprisonment.

"Anything that hurts you upsets me, and they hurt you," he said. "But I want to know *everything* about you."

Mia relaxed when he placed both hands on the steering wheel again and focused his gaze straight ahead. "Maybe another time," she said.

"No, tell me."

She stared at his chiseled, resolute profile before glancing at his white-knuckled grip on the wheel. He would deny it, but she knew if they'd discussed this before they'd had sex, he wouldn't have reacted so explosively. His eyes had stopped flashing red and become entirely blue again when he turned to look at her.

"Please, Mia."

The 'please' melted her reservations away, as did the need in his eyes.

Taking a deep breath, she braced herself before plunging in. "I was closing the coffee shop where I worked down for the night. I'd been the one staying behind to close everything down a couple nights a week for the past year. I loved the quiet of the place after everyone else left. It was peaceful, a time for myself. During those times, I didn't even mind the scent of coffee, donuts, and other human foods in the place.

"When I was done cleaning everything and counting the drawer, I set the alarm and exited onto the sidewalk. My apartment was close by, and I walked there as I always did. I could have gone in the front door of the building, but every time I came and went, I took the fire escape. At the time, I told myself it was because I wanted to enjoy the fresh air a little longer, even when it was winter time. Looking back, I realize it was really because I felt a deep-seated need to know it worked, and that I would be able to use it to escape if I ever needed it."

"In case there was another fire," he said when she grew quiet, and her gaze fell to her clenched hands in her lap.

"Yes," she murmured. "Funny how I never really realized that until now." Sighing, she lifted her eyes to his again. "The fire escape was in an alley, but I was a fully matured, purebred vampire who had survived living on the streets. I *never* worried anything could happen to me that I wouldn't be able to handle myself. I was an idiot."

"Every other vampire would have felt the same exact way. We take our strength for granted, forget that we can be brought down."

"I won't ever forget again."

"Nothing like that will ever happen to you again," he vowed.

Mia smiled at him as she eased the painful clenching of her

hands. "They were waiting for me in the shadows of the alley. I smelled them before I saw them, but I do remember that before I saw them, I had the thought the dumpsters needed to be picked up soon."

David's hands moved back and forth against the wheel. "Who was waiting for you?"

"Four of the vampires who were killed in the warehouse. At first, I was startled to see them coming toward me. It was only nine o'clock, but no one took their trash out at that time of night, and there was never anyone else in the alley. Then the odor coming from them hit me, as did the knowledge they were vampires, and that it wasn't the trash that reeked so badly."

Her nose wrinkled as the potent refuse aroma they'd emitted flooded her senses once more. "I didn't have any experience with pureblood vampires at that time. I didn't know that only we could detect the killer vampires amongst us by scent, but I knew the odor of those vampires was *wrong.* I'd encountered more than a few vampires during my time on the streets and during my many moves, but none of them had been pureblood or possessed the rotten odor of a landfill like they did.

"To this day, I have no idea how the four of them knew I was a pureblood vampire and not a turned one, but somehow they did. I'd never told anyone about my birth. It wasn't something I tried to keep secret, but I'd just never been close enough to anyone else to talk about myself or my family with them."

Those words briefly pushed aside the fury within him. Not only had she experienced so much adversity in her life, but there had also been so much loneliness. He'd never been alone. From the time he was born, he'd always had someone to love and care for him. He hadn't even been alone in his turning as Elizabeth had also turned his three best friends, ones he'd had since childhood. But Mia hadn't had anyone in years.

"You'll never be alone again."

Mia's heart soared at the promise of his words. It was such a wonderful prospect. She hadn't dreamed about having someone who would care for her again in years. Now she wanted to seize the dream with both hands and hold it close, but she was afraid she would crush it. She didn't dare hope for too much. She'd been disappointed and hurt too many times in her life to not go into things with one foot already out the door.

"I knew those vampires in the alley were off, and they outnumbered me," she continued. "I tried to flee, but three of them jumped me from behind. I fought and kicked against them as they dragged me down. They each easily had a hundred pounds on me and subdued me faster than I'd believed possible.

"At the time, I had no real idea how to defend myself against anyone. I'd carried some protection with me when I was living on the street, usually a knife, sometimes a stake. But even if I was smaller, I was stronger and faster than the humans, so a weapon was my second choice in a fight. Once I gave up my nomadic life and hit maturity, I stopped carrying anything on me. I was stupidly confident that I could handle any threat at that point."

She'd never be that stupid again. Now she could feel the reassuring weight of the stake tucked securely against her right ankle. On her left ankle, the tiny crossbow Aiden had given her before leaving the compound was holstered and loaded in preparation for an attack. Her coat was in the backseat, as she'd taken it off for the drive, but more stakes were tucked inside the inner pockets. She didn't know if David had always carried weapons on him before the warehouse, although she suspected he hadn't, but she'd watched him strap some to himself that morning.

"Once they had me pinned me down, the fourth came at me with those chains!" Now it was her turn to shake with rage as memories loomed to engulf her. Those awful chains that had been strong enough to keep a purebred vampire restrained.

"Drake was an extremely powerful pureblooded vamp," David said.

So powerful that he'd been orchestrating the capture of other purebred vampires and making money by selling their blood off to the highest bidders. Brian and Abby had destroyed him, but Drake had managed to inflict a lot of pain on others before his death.

"He must have seen you," David continued, "or perhaps one of his lackeys did, and they somehow knew what you were. There are those out there, human and vampire, who have abilities. Drake may have had someone like that working for him."

"Like Brian's mysterious ability to find people," she said.

"Yes, like that."

"You're probably right," she muttered and watched as a Mac truck went barreling by them. The force of its passing shook the car.

"Did they take you straight to the warehouse?" he asked.

Mia's chest tightened once more. This time, she didn't do her rhyming game and focus on something else; she focused on the contours of David's profile. Memorizing the curve of his cheek and the line of his jaw helped to calm her before she lost control and the panic took over.

"No, I was taken to another building first. They kept me there while they allowed others to come and feed on me." A muscle at the corner of his eye twitched. "They moved me five times before they put me in that warehouse. In the beginning, there were three other purebreds with me, different than the ones you rescued with me. I am the only survivor of the original group I was with."

David's head turned slowly toward her. She rested her fingers over his, needing the contact with him.

"I huddled in the corner, watching while they carried the body of one of those purebreds out whenever the blood loss became too much for them to take. Or—" She swallowed as her throat tightened. "—when someone became too greedy and took too much from them. I also think some of them paid for the opportunity to be able to kill one of us."

"I have no idea how long those purebreds were trapped there before I was brought in. They were too far gone to speak by the time I got there. The more time that passed, the more I wondered if this would be it, if this day would be my last. I knew—" Her voice broke.

She bowed her head as tears burned her eyes, but she refused to shed them. She would not give those pricks the satisfaction of shedding another tear over what they'd done to her. She'd cried enough while in captivity, and then again during the first couple weeks after she'd been rescued.

"I knew one day it would be me too," she said. "That one day they would be carrying my body out of there. I think they tried to keep most of us alive, since it's not like purebreds are common, but the cold and the *hunger*.... I've never been so hungry in my life. My veins felt as if they were on fire, even though I couldn't stop shivering because I was freezing from being so weak."

Unable to resist, David laid his hand over hers in order to comfort her. When she stiffened beneath him, he pulled away and gripped his hands in his lap. He was afraid that if he grabbed the wheel again he'd rip it from the car.

"The hopelessness also dragged me down, the never-ending fear, and the *pain*. In the beginning, I was determined to fight back, to get free, to inflict damage. The fight was dragged further and further out of me with every unwilling pull of my blood. The pain of that forcible blood drain didn't recede with time either. I swear it became more intense with every new bite.

"By the time they put me into that warehouse, I didn't have much left in me. I was convinced it would be the place where I died. Then one day I looked up and all of you were there. At first, I thought you'd come to feed from us too. I thought I was hallucinating, or dead already, when you freed Vicky from the wall and came back for me."

"I never would have left that warehouse without you," he grated through his clenched teeth.

"I know," she said, and she *did* know.

"I will always be here for you," he told her honestly.

She hastily wiped away the tear she'd been unable to hold back at his words. Most men would have run as fast as they could from a woman with as much baggage as her, but David made her feel as if he carried that baggage with her.

"You know, I think you might only like me because you don't have to deal with foreplay," she teased, hoping to lift the dreary mood she'd brought forth with this topic of conversation.

He blinked at her before laughing loudly. "Oh believe me, I'm going to enjoy touching and tasting every inch of you when I get the chance."

Mia's skin flushed at his words. "I look forward to it. Now let's get out of here."

He winked at her before taking a deep breath and shifting the car back into Drive. He drove along the breakdown lane before pulling onto the highway once more. Mia rested her head against the window as she watched the scenery pass by. At least six inches of snow coated the area, decorating the homes and farms set off the road. She'd traveled to Maine before, but never in the winter. There was something more serene about the land when the snow was blanketing the earth.

David's phone rang, and he answered it when Jack's name popped up on the screen. He hit the speaker button and set the phone into the cup holder. "Hey," he greeted.

"Issy just kicked me out so she can clean our house," Jack grumbled. "This woman you're bringing home better be worth the aggravation of dealing with Hurricane Issy, and the flower scents she leaves behind."

Mia did a double take at the disgruntled voice coming from the phone.

"Hello to you too, Jack," David said. "You're on speakerphone."

"Oh," Jack said, his discomfort coming through with that one word. "You could have told me that."

"You didn't give me a chance," David replied. "But then, you've always known how to make a lasting impression on women. Unfortunately for you, it's rarely a good one."

"Screw you. Issy is doing *my laundry*," Jack enunciated the last two words clearly.

"About time someone did."

"Hey there, David's lady," Jack said, apparently deciding to ignore him. "It's Mia, right?"

Mia blinked as the obviously irritated man became much friendlier sounding when he started speaking to her. David had told her about his childhood friends. He'd cautioned her that Jack could be blunt and a bit cranky, but she didn't know what to make of this guy who sounded as amused as he did annoyed.

"It is," she said.

"Nice to meet you. Sorry you're getting saddled with that asswipe for eternity," Jack said.

Mia gawked at the phone before she swung her eyes toward David. "How much did you tell him?"

"He didn't tell me anything," Jack replied. "Very few of us have ever brought a girl or guy around this bunch. We don't tend to stick with someone for long enough to introduce them to anyone, so it has to be something serious if David is bringing you here. I can't recall a single other woman he's been with who he's ever wanted me to meet."

"Shut up, Jack!" David hissed.

To his surprise, Mia started to laugh, and Jack chuckled. "At least she has a sense of humor," Jack said. "How much longer before you get here?"

"About four hours," David replied. It may be sooner, as visions of wringing Jack's neck floated happily through his mind.

"I'll make sure Issy's out of the house before then so she doesn't bother you when you get here." Before either of them could respond, Jack hung up.

"That was his way of being nice," David said as the screen on his phone went dark.

"I think being nice might have hurt him. He is amusing."

"He's something, but amusing is definitely not it," David bit out. "He's an acquired taste."

"Kind of like wine?"

"More like stinky cheese."

Mia laughed and turned to focus on the scenery again. Despite the fact she found David's easy relationship with his friends and Liam's children delightful, anxiety swirled within her. She was going to a place full of vampires she didn't know, who were all as thick as thieves. Their bonds with each other were intricate and deep. How would she ever fit in with all of that?

David would be there to help her get through it. She would be fine as long as he was there.

She hoped.

CHAPTER TWELVE

DAVID STOPPED the car in front of a thick wrought iron gate. The black fence spreading out on either side was twenty feet tall. Not only did it have barbwire going around the top, but it was also electrified. The lens of cameras glistened in the moonlight every ten feet around the fence. In between the cameras were motion detectors rigged to go off for anything weighing more than fifty pounds. With the wildlife around the area, they went off all the time, but he welcomed the heavy security now that Mia was there.

Rolling the window down, he leaned out the door and punched the code into the keypad. The gate didn't make a sound when it swung open to reveal the dirt drive beyond. Cameras turned in their direction as he drove down the lane. The red maples lining the road were all bare, but in the summer their powerful limbs shaded the drive and created a welcoming canopy.

"We moved here as a precaution against hunters after Ian and Paige met. Even with the vast number of us, we've never done anything to draw the attention of the hunters our way, but we figured better safe than sorry. After what happened with you and Vicky, Liam beefed up the security," he told Mia.

"I'm all for a lot of security," Mia said.

"So am I." After half a mile, David pulled the car to a stop in front of the old gray shingled farmhouse he shared with Jack, Mike, and Doug.

When David put the car in Park and shut it off, Mia took a deep breath and opened her door before she turned into a frozen, panicked mess who refused to exit the vehicle. She could only imagine the wonderful impression that would make on everyone if she was still sitting in the car come morning. They were here now; there was no turning back.

One step at a time. And she knew she had to take this step. David would stay away if he believed she couldn't handle being here, but he'd been doing everything to try to make her happy and put her at ease. It was time she did something for him in return. He wanted her to meet his family, and she would do it.

Mia stepped out of the car and stretched her back while she gazed at the property. Awe trickled through her at the beauty of the acres of open land that ended in thick woods, dense with pines. Across the way, the ocean sparkled with the pinks and yellows of the sun setting behind it.

From where she stood, the ocean appeared to be a good hundred feet down from the cliff at the edge of the property. The wrought iron fence across from her blocked anyone from approaching the edge of the cliff, but there was a gateway there and another keypad both inside the gate and out.

"The section of the fence by the ocean is newer. I've never seen it," David said to her. "We'd planned to keep the waterfront open until recently."

"It's still a beautiful view."

"It is," David agreed, unable to tear his eyes from her as the setting sun lit her face and eyes.

Mia focused on the main house set in the center of the sprawling property. It was a picturesque farmhouse with a farmer's porch. Christmas lights draped down from the porch roof and were wrapped around all of the poles. The glow of the

Christmas lights could be seen through the growing dusk descending over the day.

"Liam and Sera live there, with their five youngest children," David told her when he caught the direction of her gaze.

"It's so… warm," she whispered. Her own home had been warm too, with photos of all of them on the walls and her mother's collection of elephant knickknacks everywhere. Every year they'd strung Christmas lights together, decorated the tree, and hung the stockings on the mantle. She could clearly recall the last Christmas they'd all spent together, a month before her parents had died. She hadn't celebrated Christmas since.

Laughter trilled from somewhere behind the farmhouse, drawing her attention to a smaller house closer to the cliff. A petite woman with golden brown hair streaked with strands of honey passed in front of a window. Another woman with mocha-colored skin followed behind her, holding up scraps of cloth as she walked.

David stared at Mia as she gazed around the property while one of her hands rubbed at her thigh, over her burn scar. The longing on her face tore at his heart. He opened his mouth to tell her she could have all of this, that they could make a life here, but it was something she would have to learn on her own. And she would, over time.

"That's Emma and Ethan's house," David told her when Ethan walked by the window. "Emma's friends Mandy and Jill are visiting."

"Oh," Mia replied, unsure of how to respond.

"Jill and Mandy are human."

"Really? And they know about all of you?"

"They do. They come to visit often, but like the training compound, they don't know how to get here. That's more for their safety than ours."

David opened the back door of the car and removed the small suitcase and backpack within. The belongings he'd taken with him before leaving to help the others locate Vicky were inside the backpack. Mia had packed a few of the things she'd been given at the training compound into the suitcase. She could have taken more clothing, but she'd left most of it behind as few things had fit her properly, and she'd refused to let anyone buy her new things.

"I'll take you shopping tomorrow," he said as he closed the door.

She pretended not to hear him as she gazed at a Cape Cod-style house behind Emma and Ethan's, and beyond that to a double-story cottage set up near the ocean. The cottage was incredibly cute with its white paint and blue shutters. Beside it sat a matching building that was a smaller version of the cottage.

"Who lives there?" she asked when David came to stand by her side.

"Isabelle and Stefan live there with their daughter, Hope, and their son, Bodhi, or as we all call him, Bo."

"What about the cottage?"

"Ian and Paige. Before the birth of their second son, Colton, they added the second story to it. The building beside it is Paige's art studio."

"It's really cute," she said.

"It is, and Paige is very talented. Come."

He didn't touch her but nodded toward the old farmhouse with gray siding and weathered blue shutters. "It's not as cute, I know," he said as they walked toward the house, "but we are a bunch of bachelors. Or we *were*, anyway."

She swallowed heavily when his gaze raked over her. "I'm probably going to have to thank Issy for coming to clean, then," she said. "I can only imagine how neat you guys kept the place."

"We weren't complete slobs, but I'm sure Issy has greatly improved the look and smell."

The layer of salt coating the blue gray cobblestones leading to the front door crunched beneath her feet as she walked. Mia huddled deeper into the thin coat she'd taken from the compound as a chilly wind blew off the ocean and howled across the open land around them. She'd left behind the heavier winter coat she'd been borrowing in case someone else came along who would need it.

The wind caught the top coating of snow and swirled it around them. The small flakes fell against her already frozen cheeks and melted there. She'd been born in the Northeast, but this was colder than she was used to.

"Definitely getting you warmer clothes tomorrow," David muttered as they climbed the small porch to the front door.

Grabbing the door handle, he twisted it and pushed it open. Mia almost leapt into the heat emanating out of the front foyer. She hurried inside to stand before the staircase leading up to the second floor. The shadows encompassing the top of the stairs, obscured the hallway beyond.

Not only did the warmth of the house assail her, but also the fragrant aroma of lavender. Beneath the lavender, the musty smell of old wood tickling her nostrils reminded her of the home she'd shared with her parents. She'd sometimes thought that the old wood of her home held the memories of all those who had lived there before her, and those memories had scented the wood with age. It had seemed like such a fanciful notion then. It was one she'd forgotten about until now, and now it didn't seem so fanciful.

From somewhere in the house, she heard a series of shouted curses. Mia took a small step back, her gaze darting toward the door David had closed behind him. What was going on?

The accelerated beat of Mia's heart pulsed in David's ears as she gazed at the door like she was contemplating bolting through it. "They must be in the game room. It can get rowdy in there, but everyone is fine. I can take you upstairs to my room so you can rest before meeting anyone," he offered.

Mia gazed at him, then the door, and then the stairs before looking to him again. All she wanted was to run as far from there as possible, but she'd been running since she was eighteen. She'd vowed to stop doing that when she'd moved back to Connecticut, and she planned to uphold that vow. She'd asked David to bring her so she could learn more about him, his life, his friends, and because she was tired of living in fear all the time.

It was time she regained control of her life, and hiding now was not the way to do that.

Throwing her shoulders back, she tilted her chin up. "I'm ready," she declared.

David stared at her as he tried to decide how to proceed. Despite the resolute expression on her face, her distress beat against him. "Mia—"

"I will not run anymore. I am going to meet your friends and family."

The need in her eyes tore at his heart.

"Please, David."

"They're going to love you," he said, placing the suitcase and bag on the floor near the front door. He gestured toward the doorway next to the front foyer. She stepped through the door before him and into the living room.

Mia's gaze traveled over the indigo blue sectional couch positioned to face the massive TV hanging on the wall. No one would miss anything that happened on *that* TV. Dark wood beams ran across the ceiling above her, a ceiling only a couple inches over David's head.

"How old is this house?" she inquired.

"This was the first house on the property. It was built in the late 1800s. Sera and Liam's farmhouse was built in the 1970s, and the other houses are all more recent."

"I love old houses," she said honestly. "The house I lived in with my parents was from the 1800s. I always wondered about all of the people who had lived there before us. Can you imagine all the laughter and tears these walls have experienced?"

David tilted his head to study her as she gave him another glimpse into herself. "I can. You will love this house, then. Come."

He led her through the tiny kitchen with its red brick fireplace. The stove had to be at least twenty years old and was missing three of the four knobs on the front of it. The green fridge had seen better days in the 80s. Those appliances were both things that didn't matter much to vampires though, and she doubted anyone spent much time in the room. She also had a feeling the small orchid in the windowsill had been an Issy touch, and it would be dead by the end of the month if left to the care of the men living here.

"You're cheating!" someone shouted from the back of the house, and she recognized the angry voice as Jack's.

"How am I cheating?" someone else demanded.

"I don't know, but I'll figure it out, and then I'll kick your ass all the way back to your own house," Jack threatened.

"I'd like to see you try," the man speaking with Jack retorted.

"Don't tempt me," Jack said.

A harsh bark of laughter followed the declaration. Mia's step faltered as David led her out of the kitchen and down a dimly lit hall. The door at the end was cracked open enough to allow a glow to spill around its edges. The rest of the doors lining the hall were all closed, hiding whatever was behind them.

It became increasingly difficult to breathe with every step toward the door at the end, but she forced herself to continue.

One, two, three.... There was nothing nearby for her to rhyme with, and staring at the floor while being introduced to David's friends would be an awful first impression. *You can do this. You will do this!* She took another deep breath and forced herself to continue putting one foot in front of another.

"We added this back room two years ago," David said when they were a few feet away from the door.

The sound of his voice helped to ease some of the anxiety clawing at her chest.

"We all wanted a place that was off-limits to anyone under eighteen," he continued.

"The kids must hate that," she muttered.

"Of course they do, but they have their own game room, and as you can hear, this isn't exactly a place they should be."

"No, it doesn't sound like it."

"Easy, guys," a woman said. "No reason to beat each other up over poker."

"Your husband is a cheater," Jack replied.

"I resent the fact you'd accuse me of cheating my wife out of money," the man said.

"It will be *both* of your money once you leave here!" Jack shouted and laughter followed.

At the end of the hall, David rested his hand against the door. He stared expectantly at Mia, waiting for her to tell him she'd changed her mind and would meet everyone later. She certainly looked as if she were contemplating it, as her skin had paled, her lips were compressed into a flat line, and her hands fidgeted nervously with the edge of her sweater. Her head turned toward him and her shadowed eyes met his.

"We can go back," he offered.

Her lips flattened even more, and she gave a sharp shake of her head. He hesitated, but her shoulders remained resolutely thrust back.

"It will be okay," he promised. "They really are all kidding with each other. Jack's just a sore loser."

"So am I," she murmured, bracing herself as he pushed the door the rest of the way open.

She hadn't known what to expect, but her eyebrows shot into her hairline when the room beyond was revealed. Looking at the front of the house, she never would have guessed something such as this existed inside. Not even in an arcade had she ever seen so many video games. They lined the back wall of a room easily the size of the entire first floor of the house.

On the right wall, pinball machines, a mini basketball hoop, air hockey tables, ping pong tables, and other assorted games were set up and ready for someone to play with them. The left wall had a large mahogany bar with a mirror behind it. The bar sported five taps and enough liquor bottles to stock a nightclub on the shelves lining the mirror.

A man with sandy blond hair, broad cheekbones, and the build of a football player stood behind the bar, staring at the bottle in his hands. He placed it on one of the shelves before grabbing a bottle of tequila. Lifting his head, his blue eyes met hers in the mirror behind the bottles.

He stared at her for a minute before a grin split his handsome face. Mia almost clutched David's arm for support, but she kept her hands by her sides. She had to learn to stand on her own two feet before she could allow herself to lean so heavily on another. And she refused to be a clingy, needy mess in front of his friends.

The man behind the bar turned to face them as a loud groan came from her left. A poker table was set up there. Four vampires were gathered around the table. One chair was pushed back from an empty spot that she assumed had been vacated by the man behind the bar.

A grinning man leaned over the table to scoop an armful of chips toward his already large pile. The motion caused the man's black hair to fall across his forehead in waves. His emerald eyes sparkled in amusement as the other two men, and the woman sitting at the table, glowered at him.

The man laughed as he stacked his chips neatly before him. "You three have no poker face whatsoever," he told them.

"Oh, fuck off," Jack said.

She didn't know what to make of Jack yet, but Mia found herself smiling as he flipped his friend the finger before running a hand through his short, light brown hair. From where she stood, she could see the hazel of his eyes, and that, like David, his nose had once been broken and crooked a little to the side. A small bump had formed in the middle of it.

In between the two men the most beautiful woman Mia had ever seen sat facing her, while another vamp sat with his back to them. The woman finished dealing out more cards and lifted her head. Her violet-blue eyes widened when she spotted David and Mia in the doorway. The vamp who was winning leaned forward to grab his cards, but the woman grasped his wrist before he could pick them up.

Mia felt like a lab specimen when the woman gestured toward them, and all their heads turned in her direction. The one who had been sitting with his back to them twisted all the way around in his chair. Mia's fingers curled into her palms when the vampire who had turned in his seat rose to his feet and came toward them.

The man's ocean blue eyes sparkled with warmth when he

grasped David's hand and clapped him on the back as they briefly embraced. When the man stepped back, Mia got a good view of his dark blond hair and round, friendly face that could only be described as cute. He was shorter than David, but his stocky frame spoke of strength.

The man turned to her and extended his hand. "I'm Doug," he greeted.

David grabbed Doug's wrist, halting him before he could touch her. Doug's eyes flew to David as he lifted his other hand in a pacifying gesture. All smiles vanished as all eyes became riveted on David and Doug. Mia held her breath, uncertain of what was going on, or what to say as David's body vibrated with tension beside her.

Then the chair Jack had been leaning back in thudded to the floor, breaking the silence.

"Don't tell me you're going to go all batshit crazy like Liam did," Jack said, jabbing a finger at the man with most of the poker chips.

Liam scowled at him as he rose to his feet and positioned himself in front of the woman who Mia now realized must be Sera, Liam's mate. The unease in the room ratcheted up. The man behind the bar set the bottle down and walked out from behind the bar.

"No, I'm not," David said.

At least I hope I'm not. David kept those words to himself as he released Doug's wrist and stepped closer to Mia. He didn't know what to make of what had just happened. He didn't want any of his friends to upset Mia by touching her when she wouldn't welcome it, but it had been more than that. For a second, the idea of Doug touching her had sent a flood of possessiveness through him and caused a red haze to blur his vision.

David trusted Doug with his life, but he couldn't stand the idea of him anywhere near Mia. He ran a hand through his hair, tugging at the ends of it. Taking a deep breath, he composed himself once more. Liam had warned him that he'd be able to better deal with an uncompleted bond if he took it slow with Mia, but he hadn't expected his instability to control himself to start so soon after their relationship had progressed further.

I will control it.

"I'm fine," David assured everyone in the room.

Despite his words, Doug kept his hands in the air as he backed away from him.

"He is fine," Mia said, though she wasn't so certain. David had always been so confident around her, but there was a baffled look on his face that she'd never seen before. "I just... I don't like being touched."

Pride filled David when Mia admitted this to them and gazed defiantly around the room. The others in the room stared at her before glancing at him.

"Completely understandable after what you've been through," Sera said and stepped out from behind Liam.

Mia winced at the reminder that they all knew what she'd endured while in captivity. Even if David hadn't told them about what had happened in the warehouse, they would have learned it from Vicky or from the other family members who had been there when Mia was rescued.

Sera's golden hair swayed with her steps as she strode across the floor toward them. Liam stayed close to her side, his gaze focused on David as Sera stopped before Mia. Sera's eyes were kind, and the aura of warmth she exuded made it impossible for Mia not to like her instantly.

A radiant smile lit Sera's face when she spoke. "We're so happy you came. We've all been looking forward to meeting you."

Mia's shoulders sagged in relief as the others nodded their agreement. She'd had no idea what to expect from David's friends, but she believed Sera truly meant what she said.

"Thank you," Mia replied.

Sera turned to David, but when she went to step toward him, Liam moved to block her way and gave a subtle shake of his head. Mia's father had been exceptionally protective of her mother, but she'd never seen him do something like that.

"Liam," Sera protested.

Liam glanced at David before focusing on his mate again. "Not until their bond is complete," he said. "Don't argue with me on this."

Sera glanced at David and gave him a sad smile. "I'm glad you're home," she told him before retreating back to the table.

Mia almost slapped her forehead as she realized that no matter how fine David told everyone he was, they could all sense that the bond between them hadn't been completed. She could smell Liam and Sera's intermingled blood flowing through them. A vampire recognized when one belonged to another.

"We really are happy you're here," Liam said to her before taking David's hand and embracing him as Doug had. Liam smiled at her when they stepped apart, but he didn't make a move to touch her before her walked over to stand beside his wife.

"I hate this mate shit," Jack muttered, then walked over to embrace David next.

"This Mr. Sunshine is Jack," David said to her over Jack's shoulder.

"I figured that out already," Mia said with a laugh.

Jack stepped away from David. He may act like a bit of an ass, but his hazel eyes were kind when he focused on her. "Welcome," he greeted.

"Thank you," Mia replied.

"And this is Mike," David introduced as the man who had been standing behind the bar walked over to them.

"I'm the best of the bunch," Mike said to her before embracing David.

"Hardly." Jack snorted as he walked back to the poker table.

When all the greetings had been exchanged, Mia stood beside David, unsure of what to say or do next. Thankfully, she was saved from feeling completely awkward by Sera.

"How are our children doing?" Sera demanded.

Mia relaxed as David led her over to one of the barstools. She perched on it as talk turned to Vicky, Abby, and Aiden.

CHAPTER THIRTEEN

THE NEXT DAY they drove over two hours to go shopping at the mall in Bangor. Mia had repeatedly told David she would be fine purchasing some things from the closest store, but he had insisted she have a better selection. He hadn't been willing to listen when she'd offered to buy her clothes online either.

"I have no money," she protested, and not for the first time, as she watched the woods and snow covered fields flash by.

"You don't have to worry about that," he assured her again. "I have money."

"I don't like having to rely on you for everything. I have a place to stay because of you, I have—"

"Maybe it's time you start relying on someone else again. Someone who will still be here for you tomorrow and the next day. Someone you can trust."

"And I can trust you?" she demanded.

His head turned toward her, his electric blue eyes burning into hers for a second before he focused on the road once more. "Yes."

Mia didn't know what to say. She believed him; how could she not? He'd never done anything to hurt her, never lied to her. He went out of his way to protect her and not touch her. She knew it drove him crazy not to be able to hold her, but he'd never complained about it, or made her feel bad about it.

Then why was she so frightened there would be no tomorrow for them?

Because she knew how fast it could all go up in flames. She'd been there, had witnessed how rapidly a life could be ripped away from someone.

She knew she could be happy with David. He already made her far happier than she'd been since her parents' deaths. He made her body feel things no other man had, made her feel cared for in a way she hadn't felt in seven years. And it scared the hell out of her.

She inhaled a steadying breath before deciding to change the subject. "Your friends are nice."

"They are."

"They're very loving, even Jack."

He chuckled as he turned into the parking area outside of the Bangor Mall. "Yes, but he would never agree with that assessment."

Mia grimaced as she stared at the enormous building and the numerous people flowing in and out of it. A Santa stood outside the door, ringing his bell. She could already hear the Christmas music drifting out from within. At one time, Christmas had been her favorite holiday, but she'd paid little attention to it since the fire.

Now watching as the breaths plumed out of the people scurrying back and forth between their cars and the building, she felt a stirring of excitement for the holiday. If all continued to go well, she'd have someone to celebrate Christmas with this year.

"I haven't been in a mall since I was sixteen," she said.

David put the vehicle in Park at the far end of the crammed lot and turned it off. "That makes two of us."

Mia climbed out of his SUV. Mike had returned the rental car for them that morning, and they had brought David's Range Rover to the mall. Mia shoved her hands into her pockets and hunched her shoulders against the cold. Inside the inner pocket of the winter coat Sera had lent her, she felt the comforting weight of the stake against her right breast as they made their way toward the mall.

The rapid heartbeats of the numerous humans surrounding her when they walked through the glass doors caused Mia to step closer to David. She inhaled his scent as she sought to tune out the rush of blood and the sensation of being trapped within these close confines.

You can walk out at any time, she reminded herself. It didn't help to ease her escalating fear as much as she had hoped.

"Are you going to be okay with this?" he asked.

"Yes," she said and took another deep breath. "That doesn't mean I'm going to browse or try things on."

"Whatever you want." A sexy smile curved his mouth. A few of the women walking by them tripped over their own feet when they turned to look back toward him. Mia glared at them until they noticed her, ducked their heads, and sped away.

"You might want to rethink that offer. I may want to kill a few humans by the time this is over," she muttered.

"That will make two of us," he replied.

She didn't get a chance to ask him what he meant before he lightly touched her elbow and jerked his head toward the right. His hand fell away, but he remained close by her side as he walked unerringly through the crowd beside her. He somehow managed to move his body in such a way that he didn't touch her, but he also kept others from touching her too.

Though people were drawn to them both due to their inherent vampire lure, they also got out of David's way. Mia often found it interesting to watch a human's reaction to a vampire. The human's instincts said they should stay away, but they found themselves inexorably pulled toward the danger. It didn't help that David was drop-dead gorgeous, and almost every woman turned to watch him pass.

They moved swiftly down the hall toward one of the stores. Mia blinked against the glare of the lights and tried to ignore the heat of the bodies near hers as sweat beaded her forehead. Did she really need clothes bad enough to put herself through this?

Yes, she did. She couldn't deny that. She was tired of washing the same three pairs of underwear, and the one bra they'd had at the training facility that fit her. Sera had offered her more clothes, but they would all have to be rolled up and cinched in order to fit her. Sera had mentioned something about Emma being smaller too, which only made David insist that Mia have her own things.

She couldn't deny the trickle of anticipation that went through her at finally having some clothes of her own again. Even if David had to buy them for her.

She'd walked into the mall with every intention of bolting back out as soon as possible, but as they moved from store to store, she found herself relaxing. If she looked at something twice, David pulled it off the racks for her. When she realized the sheer amount of clothing he planned to buy her, she changed her mind and decided to try some of it on. She refused to waste his money by buying something that might not fit her.

"I should get something a little bigger," she told him when she opened the door and stepped out of what felt like her hundredth dressing room of the day.

"Why?" David asked as he surveyed her.

The blue sweater she wore hugged her small frame, emphasizing the swell of her breasts. Her figure was filling out as she gained weight, revealing curves that hadn't been there before. Curves that he had yet to be able to touch but knew every inch of. Curves drawing far too much attention for his liking from the nearby men who stopped to watch her as she turned before one of the mirrors. Mia remained oblivious to their attention as she carefully inspected the outfit. He did not.

A young man of about twenty-five stepped out of one of the other rooms and stopped to ogle her ass as she frowned at the mirror. David took a step closer to her, a low snarl rumbling up his throat when he caught the scent of the man's lust.

"I'd suggest moving on," David growled at him.

Mia turned at the anger in David's voice. She frowned when she spotted the human glancing nervously between the two of them. The man's gaze raked over her, causing David to move toward him. Mia hurried forward and rested her hand on his forearm before he could attack the young man. Despite the fact that David relaxed, the man paled visibly before swiftly retreating from the dressing area.

"Fucking humans," David muttered and tugged at the ends of his hair.

"The women have been checking you out all day," she pointed out as she released his arm.

"I've only noticed all of the men who have been watching you," he replied honestly.

"Good." She rose onto her toes to kiss his cheek. "But you can't eat the humans for staring."

"I can scare the shit out of them though."

She laughed as she strolled back toward the mirror outside of the dressing room. "You succeeded." She glanced around to make sure no one was near them before she spoke again. "I swear I've put on five pounds just from feeding on you these past three days. I'm almost back to the weight I was before the fire. These clothes may not fit me next month. I should get a bigger size just to make sure."

The hunger in David's eyes when he surveyed her made her toes curl. The man only had to look at her and she was ready to climb on top of him.

"Then we will buy you new clothes next month," he murmured.

"That's a waste."

"Nothing for you is a waste."

Knowing that arguing with him was pointless, she retreated into the dressing room and closed the door. She was pulling the sweater over her head when she heard the door open behind her and David's outdoorsy scent assailed her. Tugging the sweater the rest of the way off, she tossed it onto one of the chairs near the mirror taking up the entire back wall before turning to face him.

"They'll have us arrested if they find you in here," she told him.

"Like we can't change a memory or two and fix that before they take us out of here," he replied in a hoarse voice.

His teeth flashed as he leaned back on his heels before her. She wore the simple white bra she'd been wearing since the training compound, and the black peasant skirt she'd been trying on with the sweater, but his ravenous gaze made her feel as if she wore the sexiest lingerie in the world.

Everywhere his eyes ran over her, she felt as if his hands caressed her too. Her nipples puckered in anticipation, a wet heat pooling between her legs. She'd never considered having sex in a public place. With the risk of being caught, she'd been certain she wouldn't want to do it. Now she found she craved it, with him. The more her body clamored for him, the redder his eyes became.

David watched her walk toward him with an enticing sway of her hips. The irresistible scent of her arousal increased with every step she took until she stood before him.

So beautiful, he thought as she tipped her head back to look up at him. Her skin had a healthy glow to it, and her eyes were vibrant. This woman who had survived things that would have broken others was his, and he found her exquisite.

Mia rested her hands on his chest as rose onto her toes to kiss him. His fingers dug deeper into his palms until he felt blood welling within them, but he didn't dare ease his grip. If he did, he'd grab her hips, spin her around, lift her skirt, and sink himself into her.

With gentle hands, Mia guided him toward one of the chairs, undoing the button and zipper of his jeans as he walked. His breath hissed between his teeth when her hand wrapped around his swollen shaft and she pulled it free. The way she licked her lips as she gazed at his cock caused it to jump within her grasp.

When she nudged him down, David sat in the chair and gripped the seat. Stepping back, Mia reached under the skirt, pulled her underwear off, and tossed it aside. Her eyes came back to his as she lifted the skirt and settled herself so that she straddled his lap.

His fangs lengthened when the wet heat of her slid against him and her hips took up a teasing grind that had him on the verge of coming. Her eyes burned into his as he released the seat, clasped his hands behind his back and locked them around the chair.

Mia couldn't tear her eyes away from the hunger in his gaze as she reached between them, took hold of his shaft, and rubbed the head of it against her already aching center. David's eyes flashed red. "Mia," he growled.

David was obviously not in the mood to be teased, and neither was she, so Mia guided him into her. She gasped at the sensation of him stretching and filling her, a sensation she knew she'd never get used to. Her hands played with the hair at his nape as she lifted herself off him before sliding down again.

David jerked as her tight muscles drew him deeper into her. *Not deep enough.* He had to be deeper, but he couldn't grab her and drive himself into her as he longed to do. He gripped his hands so forcefully together he thought he might break one.

The movement of his hands in the mirror caught her attention and drew her eyes to the glass behind them. Her heart thudded as she watched herself lift off him before sliding down once more. In the mirror, her breasts bobbed and swayed in her bra, her eyes were heavy with passion, and her face flushed. David's head tipped back, his gaze following hers to the glass.

Leaning forward, he ran his tongue over her breastbone before scraping his fangs over one of her breasts. Mia's hips bucked against him and she moaned when his eyes locked on hers in the mirror. "You enjoy watching us?" he inquired.

"Yes... yes," she admitted breathlessly, unable to tear her gaze away from the two of them joined together in such an intimate way. Mia didn't know where this wanton creature in the mirror had come from, but she relished this part of her.

Turning his head, David licked over her skin again before nipping at her flesh. It was because of him that she found herself losing all sense of who she'd been and embracing the brazen woman he was turning her into. She wouldn't have done this with any other, but with David, it was easy to be so uninhibited. She trusted him enough to push the boundaries of her comfort zone with him.

David lifted his hips off the chair as he rose to meet her thrusting motions. Something about the sight of his body in the glass, moving in such a way and impaling her so deeply, drove her to ever higher heights as the coiling tension building within her spread out from her center to her belly. Mia nearly screamed aloud as the tension unraveled and waves of pleasure racked her body. She managed to stop herself from shouting her joy to the entire mall by sinking her fangs into his neck.

"Fuck!" David snarled before the force of her orgasm wrenched his from him.

The chair cracked as he jerked against it. Little pulses continued to contract the muscles of her sheath around him, drawing more from him until he didn't think there was any more to give. Her fangs retracted, and she licked the blood away from his neck. Her breath warmed his throat as she ran her tongue over his skin.

"Never in my life did I ever see myself doing something like that," she whispered, her lips brushing his ear.

"Neither did I," he admitted, "but you liked it."

She leaned back to give him a smile that had him hardening within her once more.

"Did I ever," she breathed.

The overwhelming compulsion to drag her against him and sink his fangs into her throat hit him. *Not ready. She's not ready!*

Right then, it didn't matter. Not to the predator within him that knew she was his, and wanted everyone else to know it too.

"David?" she asked tremulously.

His teeth grated together as his clenched jaw worked back and forth. "Don't move," he said when she went to rise off him.

Mia froze as she gazed down at him. She didn't have to see his ruby eyes to know he was struggling not to unravel before her. She could feel it in every tensed muscle of his body.

"You need to feed from me," she whispered. "To complete the bond."

She had to admit there was no denying what they were to each other anymore. He was her mate. She thrilled at the idea of it as her fingers stroked his nape. Maybe she still had some issues to work through, but she was getting better every day, and he was helping her with that. One day, she'd be a woman he could hold close. Until then, she would be the woman who could ease his frustration and his need to be joined with her for eternity.

"Not until you're ready for it."

"David—"

"No! Not until you're ready, and not in the dressing room of a mall."

"I know what we are to each other. There is no denying it. I think I can handle it. This has to be done, for you."

"This has to be done for *us*. I won't risk frightening you and possibly hurting you if you panic."

She studied the stubborn set of his jaw before releasing a sigh. "Soon."

He couldn't look at her as he nodded. The last thing he wanted was to be a disappointment to her, to somehow break her trust in him by moving too fast or doing something before she was ready, but he didn't know how much longer he could take not being connected to her completely. He'd been so certain he could hold out on binding them until she was certain she could handle it. Now he realized the choice may soon be taken from him.

"I think we're going to have to place mirrors all over the walls of our room at home," he said to distract them both from the turmoil within him.

"*Our* room?" she asked, trying to tease him back.

His eyes flashed red, and she knew instantly he hadn't been ready to be teased.

"Yes, it is *our* room, Mia."

"Yes, it is," she agreed.

A throat cleared outside of the dressing room. "Both of you please come out of there," a man commanded from the other side of the door.

Her hand flew up to cover her mouth as the color drained from her face. David leaned forward to whisper in her ear, "Get dressed. I'll take care of it."

"Are you… are you stable enough to do so?" she asked.

"Yes." He kept his hands locked behind the chair as she climbed off of his lap. Taking another minute to steady himself, he unlocked his hands, rose, and pulled his jeans up to button them. He opened the door and stepped out to face the security guard and two very unamused female employees.

The two women's eyebrows rose when they spotted him. The younger one licked her lips and giggled. The older one gave her a disapproving frown, but her eyes held an interested gleam when they came back to him. The male security guard remained anything but amused.

"You're going to have to come with me," the man said crisply to him. "As is your companion."

"No," David said in a low voice as he looked each one of them in the eye, drawing them in with his power. "Nothing happened here. You heard nothing and saw nothing." A glassy sheen descended over their eyes when they became enthralled by his words. "Go back about your day as if it were any other. Now."

The three of them bowed their heads before turning and walking away. The door opened behind him and Mia poked her head out. He'd never seen her embarrassed, wasn't sure he'd believed it possible, but her face was a fiery red hue. He could feel the heat radiating from her as she gazed between him and the door leading out of the dressing area.

"They don't remember a thing," he assured her.

Her mouth pursed as she stepped from the room with her old clothes back on, and nothing in hand.

"Where are the clothes you selected?" he asked.

"I think we're better off just going," she muttered. "Besides, you've already bought me more than enough."

"I'll take the clothes to the counter and pay for them."

"David—"

"You looked stunning in that sweater, and the skirt is a definite keeper." He would have thought it impossible, but her face turned redder. "Get the clothes and I'll take care of paying for them."

Mia retreated to the dressing room and gathered the clothes she'd set aside for purchase. Throwing them over her arm, she walked out of the room to stand beside him.

"I'm coming with you," she said.

He took the clothes and went to turn away from her, but she took hold of his hand before she could really think about it. David froze before his head turned back to her. Mia waited for her chest to constrict and her breath to leave her as she continued to hold him.

Instead, she was gripped with the overwhelming urge to start sobbing as his touch only brought her a measure of calm.

"You okay?" he asked.

"Yes."

The grin that burst over his face and the happiness blazing from his eyes stole her breath. He bent and kissed her forehead before rising away from her. She walked beside him to the cash register. She knew how well a vampire's ability to take control of another's mind worked, knew they wouldn't remember a thing, but her heart still fluttered in her chest as they approached the women behind the counter. Her face felt like it was on fire.

She'd seen more than her fair share of sex and prostitution while on the streets. Over time, she'd become immune to it all. Her embarrassment over stumbling across someone giving a blow job had faded away until she barely acknowledged it. Now she felt like an inexperienced sixteen-year-old and she had no idea why.

She glanced at David out of the corner of her eye and her blush deepened. Because he made her feel like that, she realized. He made her feel as if she were experiencing everything for the first time all over again, and she loved it.

The women behind the counter didn't notice her tomato coloring, as they remained focused solely on David. Both smiled at him when he placed the clothes on the counter. The young one fluttered her lashes in a way that caused Mia to almost punch her. Instead, she stepped possessively closer to him. The young one turned dismissively away from her to focus on the register.

When the woman was done ringing up Mia's purchases, David

paid her, lifted the bags off the counter, and carried them out of the store. "Where to next?" he asked her.

"I think I've had enough shopping for one day," Mia said.

"How about we put these bags with the others and hit one more store?" he suggested. "A store for me."

How could she tell him no when he'd spent the whole day buying her things and not uttering one word of complaint? She couldn't.

Mia walked with him out to the parking lot where he placed the bags into the back of his green Range Rover alongside the numerous others. If she didn't gain any more weight, Mia would have enough clothes for the rest of her life. Not gaining weight would probably be impossible if she kept feeding from David though. She'd never had blood as satisfying as his before, and her body was thriving on it.

"I think you spent too much money on me today," she said.

"No such thing," he told her as he reclaimed her hand. She tensed at his touch, and though she'd sought him out earlier, he waited for her to jerk away from him. Her hand remained in his as her body eased beside him, and she gave him a small smile.

Big progress, he realized. If he remained patient, it was only a matter of time before she allowed him to touch her without reservation.

He kept hold of her hand as they walked back into the mall and toward the final store. Mia gave him a disbelieving look when he stopped in front of the lingerie store. "This is for you?" she inquired.

His gaze raked over her from head to toe before he gave her a devilish smile. "Hell yes, it is."

Mia couldn't stop herself from laughing when he led her inside.

CHAPTER FOURTEEN

IT HAD TAKEN Mia a good week to learn everyone's names and to keep them all straight, but she was fairly certain she had the whole family down now. Ethan, the oldest of Sera and Liam's children, was married to Emma. They had a newborn son named Levi, after Emma's grandfather. They called him Lev.

Isabelle was their second child. She was married to Stefan and had a five-year-old daughter named Hope, and a baby son named Bodhi, or as everyone called him, Bo. Ian was the third oldest and married to Paige. They had two sons—Darius, who was four, and Colton, who was a year old.

She'd met the fourth oldest child, Aiden, at the training compound, and as they gathered around Sera and Liam's living room on Christmas Eve, Aiden smiled and waved at her from across the room. Mia waved back at him, happy to see him and Abby here.

She knew that Abby and Vicky came after Aiden in the family order. Abby had arrived with Brian and Aiden the night before, but Vicky remained at the training compound. The three of them planned to make the drive back to New York that night to spend Christmas with Vicky tomorrow. Mia knew Sera wasn't happy with Vicky's decision not to come home, but she hadn't argued it either.

Staring at Abby, Mia recalled the conversation she'd had with Sera three days prior, after Sera had found out about Vicky's decision to remain in New York.

"Vicky will come home when she's ready," Sera said. "Pushing her on it will only make her unhappy, and she's had far more unhappiness than I ever wanted her to have in her life. I just wish I could hug her again."

Mia saw the tears in Sera's eyes before she turned away from her. "She knows that," Mia assured Sera, hoping to ease some of her sorrow. "And given time, she'll move on from what happened to her. I am moving on."

"Yes, you are" Sera replied with a smile and a decisive nod. "Hopefully Vicky will soon. I miss her."

Mia was brought back to the moment when Hope squealed in delight and threw herself at Brian, who stood in the corner. No matter how much Brian frowned at them, the kids were determined to climb all over him. Hope wrapped her arms around one of his legs as she clung to him while most of the family tried to hide their laughter. Ethan and Ian laughed loudly, and Mia had a feeling the two of them had put the kids up to driving Brian nuts while he was there.

"Hope." Stefan didn't look at all amused as he walked over and pried his daughter off Brian.

"But I want to hug him!" Hope protested loudly as Stefan carried her away.

"I think you may have some competition," Issy said to Abby and elbowed her.

"I think so too," Abby replied, and Brian's glower deepened to the point where even Mia, who liked the idea of being touched by someone less than Brian did, couldn't stop herself from laughing.

Willow plopped herself down on the couch in front of Brian, draping her arms over the back of the couch and tilting her head to study him. At eighteen, Willow was three years younger than Abby and Vicky. Her eyes were a pure violet like Isabelle's, her hair a dark blonde, and she possessed the radiant beauty of her mother.

"How many vampires have you killed?" Willow asked Brian.

"Willow!" Abby blurted. "Don't you have somewhere else to be?"

"No," Willow replied blithely. "Do you?"

"Get out of here." Abby took a menacing step toward her.

Willow yelped and leapt to her feet, nearly plowing into her brother, Julian, in her rush to get away from Abby. If Mia remembered correctly, the lanky Julian, with his black hair and blue eyes, was only a year younger than Willow.

Stefan set Hope down again. She ran back over to Brian and threw herself against his leg once more. Brian's head tipped down when Hope wrapped her arms around his leg, tilted her head back, and batted her long lashes at him. He stared at the small child as if he didn't know what to make of her.

Abby bent to pull her niece off, but Brian stopped her with a hand on her shoulder. "It's fine," he said.

Abby glanced nervously between the two of them before releasing Hope. "Are you okay?" she asked him so quietly that Mia, who was only a couple feet away, barely heard her.

Brian hesitated a second before responding, "Yes."

Mia didn't understand why he wouldn't be okay with a child clinging to him, but there were many who would think she was a freak because she jumped whenever someone accidentally touched her. Everyone had their issues.

"Will you be my boyfriend?" Hope asked, her violet eyes beguiling as she peered up at Brian.

"I don't think your Aunt Abby would like that very much," Brian told her.

"She doesn't have to know."

Abby laughed and turned to Issy. "Good luck with that one," Abby told her sister.

It was Stefan's turn to scowl as he stalked over to pry his daughter off Brian once more. "You're not allowed to have a boyfriend until you're at least a hundred," Stefan told Hope as he carried her away.

Hope giggled and blew Brian a kiss over her father's shoulder. Brian blushed the color of a lobster. Isabelle and Abby laughed loudly.

"Looks like I've got some serious competition," Abby said.

"You really do," Issy agreed, and Brian pulled at the collar of his sweater.

Mia still felt thrown off by the sheer amount of vampires there, but she had to admit the family made her heart swell with joy. As did David. The endless patience he showed her, and the care he gave her, were things she'd never expected to find again in her life.

She smiled as she recalled going with him to see his boat the day before. They'd driven into town where the sailboat had been stored for the winter. Placed on stands inside a warehouse, they hadn't been able to go on the boat, but he'd still walked her around it, telling her all about it and how much he enjoyed being at sea. The excitement in his voice as he spoke had enthralled her.

Mia didn't know much about boats, but she had to admit his was pretty from what she could see of it. Running her fingers over its blue sides, she'd realized she couldn't wait for spring, when the two of them could go sailing together. She'd then realized she was thinking about things in the future with David, not focusing on the day-to-day like she'd been doing for the past seven years.

Instead of panicking over it, she'd found herself smiling as she'd listened to him talk about knots and winds. Afterward, they'd gone to the beach and settled in to watch as the stars came to life in the night sky. He'd stretched his legs out beside her and rested his hands on his thighs as she leaned her back against his chest.

She'd rattled on about the stars with the same enthusiasm he had for his boat. He listened to her, just as he'd listened to her all the other nights they'd stared up at the sky together since arriving in Maine. They had stayed on the beach until she'd been unable to take the cold anymore. Then they had returned home and locked themselves in his room for the rest of the night.

She couldn't deny that she was falling in love with him, even if it made her feel as if she'd jumped out of a plane without a parachute. She'd plummeted headfirst into this relationship with him, and she could only hope she didn't end up splattered in the end. However, she knew if there was anyone who could catch her before she hit the ground, it would be David.

She still hadn't been able to be embraced or touched by him for extended periods of time, but over the past week, she'd gradually withstood more and more contact with him.

A squeal drew her attention back to the group as Darius bolted through the crowd of vampires gathered around him. Ian bent to scoop his son up. Darius's tiny fangs were extended, his golden hair tumbled in disarray. He laughed when Ian plopped him onto his shoulder.

"Kyle! Cassidy!" Sera called down the basement stairs. "It's time to open the Christmas Eve presents! Aiden, Abby, and Brian are leaving soon!"

Mia heard the last two of Liam and Sera's children bounding up the stairs before Cassidy emerged with her twin brother right behind her. Cassidy was a little younger than Kyle, but she was the leader of the two as the twins jostled against each other to the front of the crowd.

Liam walked over, grabbed the plug for the Christmas lights, and held it into the air. Everyone followed his movement as he bent to light the fifteen-foot tree that filled the room with its pine scent. Despite the height of the tree, the angel on top didn't reach the living room's cathedral ceiling. When Liam plugged the cord in, applause erupted as red and green lights blazed to life around the tree.

A smile tugged at Mia's lips as she gazed at the colorful tree and the vast array of mostly handmade decorations covering it. She guessed most of them had been forged by the hands of Sera and Liam's children. The papier-mâché angel on the top lit up to reveal her broken wing and her twisted tilt to the right side. All of the many imperfect and loving crafts on the tree made it even more beautiful.

Sadness tugged at Mia's heart as she recalled the Christmas trees she'd had with her parents over the years. Like this one, many of the decorations on it had been created by her. Others were reminders of the years her parents had experienced as humans, before they'd met each other. More of the decorations had been from her parents' time together. Each ornament on their tree had told a story, and Mia had known all of those stories as they'd been retold every year while the three of them decorated the tree together.

Closing her eyes, she took a deep breath to rein in her grief. It was a time of celebration, not of sorrow, and she was determined to celebrate.

David felt Mia tremble as she opened her eyes to gaze at the tree. Unable to stand the distress in her eyes, he decided to give her Christmas present to her early. "I have a surprise for you," he told her.

"What is it?" she inquired.

"If I told you, it wouldn't be a surprise," he teased and bent to kiss the tip of her nose. Rising, he took hold of her hand. "But I'll show you now."

"Now?"

"Yes."

"What about everyone else and the presents?"

"They'll understand. Besides, the kids only get pajamas or slippers tonight. They won't start jumping for joy until tomorrow."

He gave her hand a subtle tug and led her out of the living room that comprised more than half the downstairs of Sera and Liam's home. The wide pine floors creaked beneath their feet as they walked to the hall. Stopping by the front door, David pulled her thick winter coat from the closet and handed it to her. He removed her scarf from the hanger afterward, wrapping it around her neck with deft fingers and securing it into place.

Mia rested her hand over her right breast, where the stake pressed against her chest. Even there, with all of the security and protection, she couldn't bring herself not to have the weapon on her.

David opened the door for her. She walked outside, and he stepped out behind her into the blustery wind. The ocean waves crashed against the shore and rolled back out again as he clasped her hand. The salty tang of the sea called to him as they hurried across the frozen snow toward the house he shared with Mike, Jack, and Doug.

If all went well, David intended to start work on a house for him and Mia in the spring. She didn't complain about sharing a home with his friends, but he wanted a place for them alone. There were many things he planned to do to her in every room of that house that he couldn't do without risking his friends walking in. Mike and Doug would both exit in a hurry, but Jack would probably sit down to watch the show.

Mia's head tilted back to gaze at the vast sky as the first star burst to life in the velvet night. She smiled as more of them illuminated the darkness. She'd assumed he was taking her home, but he detoured around it to the woods beyond.

"Where are we going?" Mia asked.

"You'll see."

She frowned at him as he led her toward a pathway in the woods that she hadn't known was there. The branches of the trees clicked over their heads as the wind blew through them while they climbed a hill. At the top of the hill, the tress thinned out a little and he led her toward the ocean.

They were almost to the edge of the cliffs when she spotted a small building that looked like a large shed, sitting a few feet away from the edge of the drop-off to the sea below. Her brow furrowed as she glanced up at David. He'd been relaxed through most of their walk, but she sensed an odd nervousness in him as he remained focused on the building.

He opened the door and moved aside to allow her to enter first. The scent of kerosene wafted to her, the heat coming out the door warming her frozen cheeks before she stepped inside. Mia's eyes widened when she took in the small structure.

A single lantern burned beside the bed that would be large enough for them both to sleep in comfortably. The bed was pushed against the right wall. The flickering flame of the lantern illuminated the room, revealing the best thing in it. Directly in front of her was a wall made of glass. Before the glass stood three telescopes, all of them pointed at the stars.

She squealed and jumped up and down before racing across the room to examine the telescopes. Her jaw dropped when she saw that one of the three was a Celestron computerized telescope. Not just any Celestron, but the top-of-the-line Pro model.

Aware of how much it cost, she'd never expected to be able to touch one. Not unless she stole it, and she hadn't stolen anything since she'd given up her nomadic lifestyle and returned to Connecticut. Once she'd decided to get her life back together, she'd vowed she would earn everything on her own from then on and not rely solely on her vampire abilities to get by, unless she absolutely required them to survive.

One day in the future, she probably would have had enough money to buy the telescope. She would live forever, after all, and she'd already started to save and invest, but it still would have been years before she ever could have justified purchasing one.

Her fingers barely grazed the telescope when she ran her hand over it, afraid to get too close for fear she might break it. She lifted her head to take in the other two telescopes. They were both amazing too, better than she ever could have hoped to obtain anytime soon, but her gaze kept coming back to the Celestron with the pretty red bow stuck on top of it.

David closed the door to the small building, shutting out the wind though the walls still rattled. The delight on Mia's face kept him fixated on her as she turned from one telescope to the next before going back to the first. She started to touch it before pulling her hands back. She clasped her hands against her chest and bounced on her toes as she tilted her head one way and then the other.

Not since Hope was given her puppy, Dawg, had he seen anyone so thrilled, yet so uncertain of something before. Mia had always seemed to be an old soul to him, one who had seen and endured far too much pain and sadness in her short life. Now her joy lit her from the inside out, giving back to her the aura of youth that had been so cruelly ripped away.

Something inside David began to shift and change as he watched Mia. Something new grew within him, making him stronger and better, for her. He cared for her, admired her strength and determination to piece herself back together after everything she'd been through over the years, but he realized he was also in love with her.

His palms flattened against the door behind him as the realization rocked him back on his heels. He couldn't tear his eyes away from her when she bent to examine the telescope more closely, but still didn't touch it.

"It's yours, you know," he said around the lump in his throat. "You can touch it."

Her head shot around to him, her mouth parted as she shook her head in fierce denial. "It's too expensive. I can't accept this."

"Too late. It's been paid for, and I don't know how to use it, so someone has to. Otherwise, it will sit here and rot."

Mia gawked at him as she tried to process his words. "It's almost a ten-thousand-dollar telescope."

"I know."

"You can't let that rot."

He laughed. "I can. *You* can't."

"David—"

"It's yours, Mia. So are the other two, and if you would prefer a different one, I'll buy that one for you too."

"No!" she blurted, her fingers fell to caress the telescope before her in a loving manner. "No. This one… this one has been a dream for a while," she murmured as she turned back to it.

"A dream, huh?"

"Oh yes." She walked around the telescope, examining every inch of it, but she didn't take her fingers away from it again. "A very big dream."

David watched as she knelt next to it before moving to look through the eyehole at the stars beyond. She seemed to forget he was in the room as she adjusted this gadget and then that one. He was fine with that as it gave him a chance to relish the joy he'd been able to give her. Striding over to the bed, he kept his eyes on her as he sat on the edge of the mattress and bent to untie his boots. Putting his toes against the heel of each boot, he kicked them off and removed his socks.

"Everything is so clear. It's almost like I can touch the moon," she breathed. When she was done fiddling with that telescope, she shed her coat before moving onto the second one. "Damn good taste in telescopes," she muttered.

"And women," he replied, but she didn't appear to hear him.

"It's Mercury!" she declared. "The Big Dipper and Orion."

He'd come to know the names of the constellations more since she'd entered his life, but he still found himself listening in fascination as she switched to the next telescope.

"Cassiopeia!" she cried.

David swung his legs onto the bed and leaned against the wall of the small structure he'd worked to build with Mike, Doug, and Jack the day before, while Mia had been with Sera. It was small enough that it only took them a couple hours to assemble and secure, but he planned to get a lot of hours of enjoyment out of it until the spring.

Sera had given him the things to decorate the room with, which had been more pillows than he ever would have put on his bed and a deep gray comforter with matching sheets. The only other thing in the room was the kerosene heater in the corner and blinds that could be lowered over the glass wall facing the ocean.

David propped his hands behind his head. He couldn't help but smile as Mia prattled off more names of constellations and stars. She shed her scarf, boots, and sweater as she continued to move between each telescope. Her eyes shone a bright blue against the black turtleneck she wore, and her skin glowed with vitality as she skipped back to the first telescope. He'd have spent millions of dollars to bring this kind of happiness to her over and over again.

"The Milky Way is *right there*! We have to bring all of these telescopes with us when we go to see the Northern Lights. Oh, and the

Southern Cross! We definitely have to see the Southern Cross! We have to see the stars from *everywhere*!"

He didn't know if she was aware that she was talking about their future, but he was. His heart beat faster, his fangs elongated, and his dick swelled with his need for her. But he didn't interrupt her as she bounced from one telescope to the next over and over again, exclaiming at each new star or constellation she found through the eyepiece of each.

CHAPTER FIFTEEN

THE STARS WERE FADING from the sky when Mia took a deep breath and finally stepped away from the telescopes to gaze out the window. He thought she might have just become aware of the ocean sprawled out before her when she tilted her head down to gaze at the waves. David stared at her reflection in the glass as she rested her fingers against it to peer down at the water below. From their new home, she would have her sky, and he would have his sea.

Mia turned and smiled as she took in David's spread-out form on the bed. Her eyes were drawn to his obvious erection, and her skin prickled with anticipation of what he craved. "You could have interrupted me," she told him.

"Your happiness is more important than mine."

Tears burned her throat and eyes as his words sank in. "I can't ever thank you enough for this."

"Watching you enjoy them was more than thanks enough."

"Oh really?" she inquired mischievously. "You wouldn't like something a little more satisfying than that?"

"And what do you have in mind?"

She prowled toward him, her hips swaying with each step she

took. The past week had put more weight on her. The undernourished vampire they'd pulled from the warehouse had vanished, and in her place was a woman with rounded hips and breasts that would fit his hand perfectly when he was able to cup them.

Her hands slid down the front of her turtleneck to grip the edge of it. With deliberate, sensuous movements, she slid it up her belly to her breasts before pulling it over her head. His breath sucked in when she revealed the lacy red bra that exposed more of her breasts than it covered. The barely there bra pushed her breasts invitingly high and revealed the hardened nubs of her nipples. He clearly recalled the bra from her purchases at the lingerie store, but he'd yet to see it on her.

Slowly her hands slid down to her jeans. She undid the button and slipped them down her hips, her thighs, and then her calves before stepping out of them and kicking them aside. The matching red underwear had silken straps crisscrossing over her hips and around to her taut ass.

His hands clenched behind his head as she strolled toward him, her hands sliding up to cup her breasts before her thumbs rubbed over her nipples. He growled when she knelt on the bed beside him and swung her leg over so she straddled both of his.

"You like it when I touch myself in front of you, don't you?" she inquired as she moved up his body so her breasts were mere inches away from him.

"I do."

"Hmm," she murmured as she gripped the edge of his sweater and tugged it up over his abs. He lifted his arms above his head so she could pull it off and toss it aside. Mia drank in the sight of his bare chest and chiseled abs. She'd come to know every detailed inch of him, yet each time she saw him, he took her breath away.

Scooting back, she undid his button and slid his jeans down his muscular legs. The crisp blond hair on his legs tickled her fingers as she worked at undressing him. She tossed his jeans aside and took a minute to just gaze at his naked, masculine beauty and the proud shaft standing up from his body in eager anticipation of being buried within her.

Slowly, her gaze came back to his. Behind his lips, she saw the outline of his extended fangs. She could feel how badly he needed her, yet he'd locked his hands behind his head again in order to keep from touching her.

Rising to her feet, Mia slid her panties off and tossed them aside before unclasping her bra. There would be nothing between them, not tonight. She wouldn't allow there to be. Climbing back onto the bed, she moved so she straddled his hips once more. The head of his cock rubbed against her aching center, but she didn't take hold of him and guide him into her.

She leaned forward until her breasts brushed his chest. His breath hissed in, and she nearly jumped out of her skin at the electrifying contact of his flesh against her sensitive nipples, but she didn't pull away. Instead, she moved closer until they were skin to skin, from her breasts to the thighs she pressed against his legs.

It was the most skin contact they'd ever had. His eyes searched hers as she inched closer to him until their breath intermingled. His eyes remained riveted on her. The muscles in his forearms bulged, beads of sweat dotted his forehead, and a muscle in his jaw twitched as he fought to keep from grabbing her.

Her love for him grew as they stared at each other, his blue eyes burning into hers. Her breasts rubbed against his chest as she slid up to enclose her hands on his wrists. She gave them a tug, but he kept them locked together.

"If I'm going to control myself, they stay where they are," he said.

"Don't control yourself. I want *you* to touch *me* now."

His body became as still as stone beneath hers. They gazed at each other for a long minute. A minute in which every accelerated beat of his heart sounded loudly in her ears. In which she knew he did not breathe.

"Mia?"

"Make love to me, David," she whispered and tugged at his wrists again.

She felt whatever control he'd been retaining snap like an elastic band stretched too far. Bracing herself, she waited for him to pounce on her and take from her everything he'd been denying himself these past weeks. It would frighten her, but she would withstand that fear. She could do anything for him.

He didn't pounce though. Instead, his hands clasped hold of her cheeks, and he emitted a groan as he held her with a tenderness she'd never experienced from a man before. Especially not from a man who desired her as badly as David did.

His eyes continued to hold hers when he bent his head and placed the gentlest of kisses against her lips. The tears she'd been holding back spilled down her cheeks as something primitive and true burst forth within her. She loved him. And that love burned hotter than the sun through her.

"Don't cry," he whispered against her lips as he brushed away her tears with his thumb.

"I can't help it," she choked out. "I… I love you."

His eyes sparkled as he gazed at her. "I love you too."

More tears slid free as she wrapped her arms around his neck. His hand clasped the back of her head before he claimed her mouth. His tongue slid over her lips and then slipped inside to take possession of her mouth in a kiss that claimed her as his. She mewled in pleasure and wiggled over him as she sought out his shaft. She wanted nothing more than to feel him inside of her.

He held back from entering her while his other hand cupped one of her breasts. The sensation of his warm, strong hand kneading her flesh nearly caused her to climax right then. It had been years since she'd felt someone else's hands on her in such a way, and her long-deprived body begged for more of his touch.

She jerked in his grasp when his thumb rolled over her nipple before pinching it. He moved to fondle her other breast, his hips surging up so the rigid length of him rubbed teasingly over her clit, but he still didn't sink himself into her.

"Better than I ever dreamed," he murmured against her mouth while his hands moved steadily lower over her body. His knuckles grazed her sides as he stroked her leisurely up and down.

Mia moaned when his fingers slid between her thighs. She pushed her hips forward, rubbing against him as he stroked her, but didn't penetrate. Touch had been a thing of dread for so long that she hadn't believed it possible for someone to make her feel so courageous and aroused by it again, but David did.

Her body begged for release from this delicious torment as he slipped a finger into her. Mia rose onto her knees when he began to move his hand back and forth within her, rubbing her clit with each deliberate thrust of his palm.

His mouth fell to her breast at the same time he slipped another finger within her. The sensations were almost too much to bear as his fingers moved within her while his tongue laved her nipple. Her head fell back as she rode his hand.

The scent of Mia's arousal engulfed him, driving him to higher heights of passion, yet he couldn't stop caressing her, tasting her. He'd been denied too long; he needed more of her flesh against him, beneath him, around him. Her wet heat enveloped him as her cries sounded in his ears.

His control frayed when her head fell back, and her hands rested on his shoulders. "I can't.... I have to...."

Unable to get words out anymore, he pulled his hand away from her and flipped her over on the bed. Mia's eyes flew open when he drove himself into her. For a second, he was completely lost to the powder blue of her eyes. Her hand flattened against his cheek as they gazed at each other before he pulled back and slid into her again.

Her hips rose to meet his as he buried himself inside her. The weight of his body and the sensation of his skin on hers engulfed her until she couldn't tell where he ended and she started. She was lost to him as they were joined together, and she welcomed it. Her fingers curled into his back, pulling him closer. She didn't consider panicking at having someone else touching her so completely. Instead, she couldn't get enough of feeling him all over.

His muscles flexed and bunched beneath her hands. She reveled in his body moving over hers as he pushed her closer and closer to the brink. She locked her legs around his waist as she rode out the storm of his body's possession of hers. Turning her head, she bit into his neck and welcomed the hot wash of his blood filling her mouth.

David locked his arm around Mia's waist and lifted her against him as he drove relentlessly into her. His fangs throbbed to feast on her, to finally know what it would be like to taste her. Unable to hold back anymore, he sank his fangs into her shoulder. Her fingers dug into his flesh, but she didn't try to pull away from him or tell him to stop as her potent, purebred blood filled him.

The rightness of her blood poured into his cells as her power flooded him. Against his neck, Mia cried out as her body came undone beneath his. He thrust into her again and gave himself over to the exquisite sensation of her sheath clenching around his cock. His body shuddered as his release poured into her while her blood continued to fill him. Never in his life had he tasted something as sweet or as strengthening as her.

Mia couldn't get enough of the emotions battering her. She was swept away by the amount of love he had for her as the pathways between their minds opened, the bond between them solidifying into something she felt she could almost reach out and touch.

Mated. She felt it all the way to the center of her soul, to the very core of her being. She suddenly understood her parents' intense bond. She'd always believed she understood it before, but now she *truly* did. She belonged to him, and he belonged to her.

David reveled in feeling her mind as it entwined with his, and they became joined for all eternity. Her love spilled over him, warming him more than the sun on a hot July day. Leaning back, David lifted her off the bed. She kept her legs around his waist as he cradled her against him. Her tears spilled down to wet his skin, but he knew they were tears of joy as the emotion poured from her and into him.

David lost himself to her as she moved over him again.

THE SUN WAS POURING through the glass window and creeping

toward the bed when Mia lifted her head from David's chest. She ran her fingers over his face before tracing the bridge of his nose and the bump there. "How did you get this?"

He smiled at her as he caught her fingers and pressed a kiss against them. "When Jack and I were twelve we were walking home from school after detention. A group of high school kids started harassing us and we ended up getting into a fight with them. There were five of them and just the two of us. We both ended up with broken noses, black eyes, and a whole lot of scrapes and bruises, but we also inflicted enough damage on them that they never bothered us again."

She couldn't help but chuckle over the pride in his voice and on his face. "So it was worth the hurt then?"

"It was."

Turning from him, she finally took the time to examine the small building. "Whose place is this?"

"Ours, for now," David replied as he traced the delicate curve of her spine with his fingers. Now that he could touch her, he couldn't get enough of feeling her silken skin and warm body.

"Ours?"

"Yep. It's our new home."

"I've definitely had *far* worse accommodations over the years."

David kissed her forehead and nuzzled her hair. "Well, it's the site of the new home I'll build for us in the spring. Until then, we can retreat here when we want to get away from the house."

"Really? You plan to build us a home?"

"Yes, with a lot of help. All of us went in on buying this land together. There's over a hundred acres here, and I've claimed this piece of it for us."

Her eyes lit up nearly as much as they had when she'd seen the telescopes. He almost laughed out loud when he realized where her priorities were. Stars, number one; home, number two.

"A home," she breathed. "It's been so long."

"A home. And I'm thinking we can make the wall facing the ocean all windows. Tinted of course, so we can see out, but no one can see in. I have plans to make the windows almost like mirrors where I can watch you all the time."

Mia's breath caught at the promise of his words. "Brilliant idea."

"And we'll put an observatory at the top, for you."

She flung her arms around his neck. He inhaled her rose scent as well as the potent aroma of his blood coursing within her while he held her close. The bond between them was complete. Being mated wasn't something he'd really considered for himself. It wasn't something he'd dreaded happening to him either, like Jack, but he'd also known it was something that might never happen to him.

It had happened though, and there wasn't a thing he would do to change it.

"My present for you is nowhere near as lavish as these telescopes and a house," she whispered in his ear, sounding almost ashamed. "I wanted to buy you something for your boat, but…."

But she hadn't had the money, and despite their bond she still felt as if she had nothing, he realized. He'd been so focused on finding spare time to help Jack, Mike, and Doug get everything for this place set up that he hadn't stopped to think she would want to buy presents for others too, and that she wouldn't have the money to do so. It was something he would soon remedy.

"Everything that's mine is yours too, Mia."

"David—"

"I've done well over the years. We all have. Between buying and selling real estate, stocks, bonds, funding tech companies and medical companies, I've made a lot of money, and it's yours. I was so busy concentrating on getting this ready for you in time for Christmas that I forgot to think about you. I'll give you the information for my checking accounts. You'll have access to those funds today, and sometime soon we'll sit down and go over everything else together."

"I can take care of myself," she replied and cringed when pain slashed across his face. "I didn't mean it to come out like that. You have to understand that I've only had myself to rely on for years now. It's difficult for me to learn and accept something different. I'm not used to having another to rely on and I don't want charity. I want to earn things for myself."

"I do understand that," he said quietly. "But now it's time for you to experience something different. This isn't charity, this is us building a life and a future together. I'm inside you, and you're inside me for as long as we live. You're my mate, Mia."

"Yes, I am," she whispered as she tenderly kissed his lips. "It's going to take me some time to adjust to having someone to count on again, and to not have to worry about how I'm going to make it through every day, but I will."

"I know." He pulled back to look at her. "Besides, a Christmas present doesn't matter. You're the best gift I've ever gotten."

"I believe you, but everyone should have something to unwrap on Christmas."

"You can put on every piece of lingerie you own throughout today and I will *gladly* unwrap you over and over again."

She laughed as she gripped his shoulders. "I can do that, but I think we should get back to the others now. Those kids have to be dying to open their presents."

Sera had told her the day before that they would wait until all the family was gathered together before opening the presents. She knew that included David, and now her.

David eased his grip on her and set her down on the mattress. "Damn kids," he muttered.

"You wouldn't know what to do without them."

"I wouldn't," he admitted as he slid to the end of the bed and rose.

Mia bit her lip as she watched him stalk over and snag his jeans off the floor. Every muscle in his body flowed with supple grace as he moved. His ass was so firm she could bounce a quarter off it, and she decided to give it a try tonight. Her hands itched to hold him again, to feel him moving over her as he had early this morning, but if she did that they would never leave here.

Mia tore her gaze away from him and climbed out of bed to

retrieve her clothes. "There's somewhere I'd like to go tomorrow," she said as she slid her bra on.

"Where?" David asked.

Mia stared at the slats of the wooden floor before lifting her head to look at him. "You'll see."

David frowned, but he didn't push her on it. She would let him know when she was ready. "Then we will go."

CHAPTER SIXTEEN

MIA TOOK the mugs of steaming hot chocolate from Sera and set them on the tray next to other mugs Sera had made.

"This is a habit left over from my human days," Sera said to her. "It never seems like Christmas until I've had some hot cocoa. David and I may be the only ones who still drink it, but I always make enough for everyone."

Sera's eyes twinkled as she handed Mia another mug. "I don't suppose you've ever tried it?"

"I haven't," Mia admitted. "But it does smell better than a lot of other human foods I've encountered."

"That's the chocolate, and the marshmallows. You should try a sip. If you've never had chocolate, you're missing out."

Mia stared at the mug in her hand and sniffed cautiously at the thick brown liquid inside. Sera wouldn't steer her wrong, but she'd never eaten human food before. Though she supposed technically it was a liquid, and she'd tried alcohol before. The alcohol hadn't been too bad, but this brown stuff with the white puffs floating in it made her a little uncertain.

She glanced up as Sera turned away and removed a tray of

cookies from the oven. The cookies smelled good, but Mia wanted nothing to do with the Santa shapes on the cookie sheet. The smoky scent of the crackling fire drifted into the kitchen to mingle with the aromas of the sugar cookies and chocolate.

"Does anyone eat those?" she inquired.

"No," Sera sighed. "Not even me anymore, but it wouldn't be Christmas without the smell of them. I started baking them with oats a while ago. The kids throw them outside for the deer at the end of the day."

Sera closed the oven and wiped her hands on her apron. Mia was closer in age to Sera's children, and all the kids were friendly and welcoming, but the siblings' bonds with each other were extremely tight. Sera was their mother, and though she looked the same age as her children, and they were closer than most families Mia had encountered over the years, Sera maintained that motherly role.

Sera had friends there, with the Stooges, but Mia sensed that Sera had also been missing out on having a friend of her own. One who was separate from her husband's childhood friends, and her children's mates.

Mia had never really had a friend, but she'd started to consider Sera one. She welcomed Sera's warmth and openness in her life. She hadn't realized she'd been craving a friend to talk and laugh with over the years until now.

Mia blew on the steam wafting up from the mug and took a cautious sip of the liquid. Her lips pursed when it filled her mouth. She tried to swallow it down, but her throat closed against it. Leaning over the mug, she discreetly spit it back in.

She lifted her head to find Sera watching her with her lips compressed, her face turning red as she tried not to laugh. "Just like my kids. No taste." Sera chuckled and took the mug from her to pour it down the sink "Apparently purebred vampires have no appreciation for sweet things."

"Is that what you consider sweet?"

"Yeah," Sera said as she lifted another mug, blew on it, and took a sip. "At one time, it was definitely sweet."

"And now?"

"Now I'm not sure," Sera admitted with a sigh.

"I'll take the tray into the other room for you, if you'd like?" Mia offered.

"No, even David didn't take more than a sip of it last year." Sera placed her mug on the counter as a burst of laughter erupted from the living room. "But they'll all still drink the eggnog, if I pour enough rum into it."

"Rum would make the hot chocolate go down better too."

"Maybe one day I'll let the last of these human things go."

"Don't," Mia said. "Traditions are good."

"They are," Sera agreed. "And you'll be a part of them from now on."

"At least next year, I'll know not to try the hot chocolate."

Sera laughed and leaned her hip against the counter. "I'm glad you've completed the bond. Liam will let David near me again now."

"They are possessive," Mia said, "and protective."

"Are they ever!" Sera agreed as the haunting melody of a Christmas Carol began to play on the baby grand piano in the living room. Mia didn't know who was playing the song, and she couldn't place it, but it was beautiful. "Come on, maybe we can talk Cassidy into singing for us. She may be my devil child, but she sings like an angel. No idea where she got her voice from either. She got the devil spirit from her father though."

Mia laughed and walked out of the room with Sera. Her eyes instantly found David, standing near the fireplace with Liam, Jack, and Mike. Her heart gave a stuttering beat. She didn't think she'd ever get used to seeing him and knowing he belonged to *her*. His mouth quirked in a sexy smile when he spotted her. Her fingers itched to brush away the strand of blond hair falling boyishly across his forehead and into one of his eyes.

Nope, she would never get used to seeing him, or the way he could make her toes curl with a smile.

David stopped speaking mid-sentence when Mia stepped out of the kitchen, and his gaze fixated on her. He'd never seen her look more radiant than she did with the color high on her cheeks and her deep red sweater hugging her body. The scent of his blood flowing through her cut through all the other aromas in the room.

"Ugh, I hate this mating shit," Jack muttered from beside him, breaking the spell Mia cast over him every time David saw her.

Mike laughed while Liam and David gave Jack dark looks. "I can't wait for it to happen to you," Liam said.

"Bite your fucking tongue. I'll never be some whipped sap who gets led around by a woman," Jack replied, then walked over to stand beside the piano as Doug continued to play, "O Come, O Come, Emmanuel."

"If Jack finds his mate, I hope she leads him around by his balls," Liam said.

David nodded his agreement. "His tongue would be preferable."

"Maybe we'll get lucky and she won't let him talk," Mike said.

"One can hope," Liam replied, and the three of them laughed.

"I would *love* to see it happen to him," Mike said, taking a sip of his eggnog.

"What about you?" David asked.

Mike shrugged, but a look of longing crossed his face before he quickly composed his expression once more. David suspected being mated was something Mike might enjoy, or want. Over the years, Mike had always seemed content to go from one relationship to the next, but there was something in his eyes now that David had never seen before. Mike lowered his arm off the mantle and straightened away from the fireplace.

"I'm glad it's been settled between you and Mia," Mike said to him.

"For the most part," David said. "There will still be things to deal with, but…."

David's attention was drawn back to Mia as she made her way toward him. She still avoided bumping into anyone, but her body was nowhere near as rigid around others as it had once been. A smile lit her face when she stopped to speak with Paige and Emma for a minute.

"But?" Liam prodded.

"But she's mine and nothing will ever change that." David hadn't meant the words to come out as a growl, but they did.

"No, it won't." Liam clapped him on the shoulder and gave it a squeeze. "You're in for one hell of a ride."

"I'm looking forward to it," he replied as Mia continued toward him.

He opened his arms to her, she slid into his embrace and encircled her arms around his waist. She rested her cheek on his chest and hugged him. No one had commented on her touching him so openly, but David knew it hadn't gone unnoticed.

David rested his chin on her head and gazed around the room as Sera guided Cassidy toward the piano. Cassidy scowled at her mother, but she reluctantly stepped up to the piano and bent to speak into Doug's ear. Doug finished the song he was playing before beginning "O Holy Night."

Everyone within the room froze, and even little Lev stilled in Emma's arms when Cassidy's voice filled the air. Mia's heart leapt into her throat as the lanky, young girl started to sing. She'd never heard a voice so lovely and pure before. Tears pricked at her eyes as Cassidy's voice rose higher to fill the room with its haunting beauty.

When the last note faded away, everyone remained unmoving and hushed until a log in the fire popped. Then a raucous round of cheers and clapping erupted around the room. Cassidy crossed her legs and gave a sweeping bow before switching her leg position and doing it again. Her pretty face glowed as her blue eyes surveyed the room.

"Sing, "Frosty the Snowman" next!" Hope yelled.

Helpless to do anything but obey, Doug began to play and Cassidy started to sing once more. Mia pressed closer against David as happiness encompassed her. This was her family now. It was time she said good-bye to her past and embraced her future.

MIA ROSE from the bed and walked over to the telescopes facing the wall of glass. Behind her, she heard David shift his weight as he sat up on the bed. "What are you doing?" he asked.

"Getting your gift."

"I'm pretty sure you've gifted me right into dehydration these past couple hours," he replied.

Glancing over her shoulder at him, she was unable to stop herself from laughing at the satisfied smirk on his face. "You pounced on me before I could give you your present, and Christmas is over now."

"I didn't hear any protests from you when I pounced."

"That's because I like it when you pounce."

"Damn right you do."

Mia bent to press her eye to the eyepiece of the telescope. She adjusted it to point toward Ursa Major. From there, she searched out a small star to the right of the constellation and focused on it.

"Come here," she said, then stepped away from the telescope.

Rising to his feet, he stalked toward her. The predatory glint in his eyes had her biting her bottom lip to keep from pouncing on *him*.

"Aren't you tired?" she asked as his cock stiffened with every step he took.

"I was, until you bent over in front of me. You have an irresistible ass."

"You *are* an irresistible ass," she retorted.

His teeth flashed as he stopped before her. Mia's gaze ran over his honed body until she had to tip her head back to look up at him. He was magnificent, and every inch of him was hers.

"I am," he agreed.

Mia rolled her eyes and waved at the telescope. "Take a look."

Bending, he placed his eye against the lens. "The Big Dipper."

"Yes. Do you see the small star in the center of the telescope?"

"I do."

"That's yours."

He stared through the lens for a second longer before rising to peer questioningly down at her. "I have a star?"

"Yes."

Mia clasped her hands behind her back, her fingers fiddling anxiously as she watched him. The stars were more her thing than his, but she'd wanted to do something for him for Christmas. She had some money in her bank account, but she hadn't dared to touch it. She had no idea how much the vampires who had taken her prisoner knew about her, and she wasn't about to risk them finding her somehow. Instead of using her own money, she'd applied for a credit card under a fake name, fibbed about her yearly income, and bought a star for him.

At the time, paying off the card had been a problem for another day, but David had given her access to his bank accounts before they'd come to their secluded spot again. After she'd gotten over the staggering amount of money in those accounts, and the realization that he really did want her to spend that money, she'd paid off the credit card and set up a large, monthly donation to the nearest shelter specializing in homeless teens. As soon as she was more settled, she would start volunteering at that shelter as often as she could.

"Yes. I… I had it named after you. I know you're not really into stargazing," she blurted out. "And next year—"

Her words were abruptly cut off when he wrapped his arms around her and lifted her off the ground. He strode across the room to the bed with her locked against his chest.

"It's perfect," he told her. "Every time you look at the stars, you'll be thinking of me, looking for *me*. And you look up there pretty often."

"You really like it?" she asked as she rested her hand against his cheek.

He turned to nuzzle her palm with his lips. His happiness thrummed through the bond connecting them as he lifted his head from her hand and bent to nibble at her bottom lip. "I love it. You gave me a star."

His tongue swept leisurely over her lips before sliding in to take possession of her mouth.

CHAPTER SEVENTEEN

DAVID DIDN'T ASK where they were going as Mia drove out of Maine and into New York. She hadn't said their destination, but before they crossed over into Connecticut, he had begun to suspect her intent as her body became increasingly tensed and she stopped speaking with him. Stretching his legs out, he watched as homes and trees passed by in a blur before they entered a small town.

Despite the chill of winter, there were a few people strolling leisurely up and down the street and ducking into stores. The diner on the corner was packed with the lunch crowd. Cars lined the street as people sought to enjoy the rest of their holiday time off. At the rotary in the center of the town, a group of children was busy rolling a giant ball for a snowman. Their laughter filled the air as their breaths plumed around them. Mia drove them by a movie theatre and a fast food place before passing a small strip mall.

"It's different than it used to be," Mia murmured as she gazed at the town that was so familiar yet strangely not. "More built up."

David glanced over at her but she remained focused ahead, and he knew she wasn't talking to him. He rested his hand on her knee, causing her to start. She didn't jerk away from him though. Her gaze came toward him; a smile tugged at the corners of her mouth.

She turned her attention back to the road as they drove out of the town and down a tree-lined street. He caught only glimpses of houses through the trees. If there had been leaves on the trees, he never would have been able to see what little he did of the roofs and chimneys.

Mia made a right-hand turn onto a two-lane road. David didn't see any homes through the bare trees pressing close against the road anymore, but he did spot a couple deer making their way through the woods. After about a mile, Mia made another turn onto a dirt driveway.

The springs in the Rover bounced as she drove over the ruts in the road. Ice crunched beneath the tires when she slowed the vehicle to a near crawl, not because they couldn't navigate the road faster but because David could feel her dread increasing with every passing second. She hunched farther over the steering wheel, her knuckles turning white as she kept her eyes locked straight ahead.

Then the trees gave way to reveal a white house sitting in the middle of a couple acres of open land. Mia's breath exploded from her. She hadn't known what she would expect to find there—the charred remains of her home, a clearing, or absolutely nothing. She'd never considered that someone would have built a *new* home where hers had once stood.

Behind the house, horses moved around a paddock munching on the hay that a woman was tossing out to them. A small squeal drew Mia's attention to the two children who bolted out the backdoor and toward the barn.

"We didn't have a barn or horses," she murmured. "And our house was yellow, a cheery yellow, not an ugly one. My mom loved the color yellow. She said it brightened her mood and made her feel as if the sun was shining, even at night."

They were the most inane comments, but she couldn't quite process everything she was seeing. She'd thought the town had changed. This was a whole new world, and yet it was a world that was unsettlingly familiar. Her home had been a colonial; this one was a farmhouse with a wraparound porch.

However, despite all the differences in the homes and landscapes, she began to pick out familiar things.

"I used to play in that tree, over there," she said, pointing to the large oak with its sweeping boughs. "And that pathway through the woods back there, it leads to a lake. In the winter my dad and I would go skating on it. Neither of us was very good at it, but we always had fun."

"I bet."

Her hands clamped hold of his as she sought to ground herself in the present while the memories of the past threatened to bury her. "I'm glad… I'm glad it's not a burnt-out basement or an overgrown field, or whatever else it could have become. I'm glad life has continued here. And the family seems happy."

"They do," David agreed as the woman approached the fence to stare at them. The screen door opened and a man stepped onto the front porch. "They've noticed us. Do you want to get out and look around?"

While they'd been driving, she'd been determined not to get out of the vehicle, just to take a peek, say her good-byes to the past, and leave. Now, she found her hand falling to the door handle, and she pushed the door open. Reaching behind her, she removed her coat from the backseat and slipped it on before climbing out of the SUV. Her hand instinctively touched upon the stake in her inner pocket as the man and woman walked toward them. Sniffing the air, Mia realized the coppery scent of their blood was that of humans.

David climbed out the passenger side and walked around to take hold of Mia's hand. The man said something to the woman when they met in the center of the yard. The woman turned to call to the kids, who ran up to them. The man knelt and adjusted the coat of the little boy before the boy nodded and dashed up the stairs to return inside.

Rising to his feet, the man took hold of the woman's hand as the little girl ran back to stand by the fence. She gazed curiously at them but didn't come any closer.

"Can I help you?" the man inquired when the couple stopped in front of her and David.

"I... uh... I'm sorry to bother you, but I used to live here," Mia said. "Well not here, in this house, but on this land."

"Oh," the woman said. Then "Oh," with far more sadness in her voice and wider eyes.

"The house on this land before us caught on fire," the man said, and the woman shot him a pointed look.

Mia couldn't stop herself from wincing at his words. "Yes, it did."

The man cringed when he realized that it had been Mia's home. "I'm sorry," he murmured, and the woman shook her head at him.

The man's gaze ran over Mia before he turned back to the porch just as the little boy stepped outside again. The man waved to the boy, who jogged down the stairs toward them. Small and nimble, Mia would have guessed the boy to be about ten. The boy stopped beside his dad for a second and then turned to smile at them.

"Hello!" he greeted happily.

"Hi," Mia said, grateful for the distraction from her memories and the couple.

"I like your car."

David turned to look at the Rover before focusing on the family again. "Thank you," he said to the boy.

"Why don't you go play, Kip," the woman said and ruffled her son's blond hair.

Kip nodded and darted away. He ran around the Rover, rising on his toes to peer into the windows before running around to the back of it again. With a giggle, Kip raced past them to where his sister stood by the fence. The boy scrambled through the rails of the fence and the children both ran in and out of the horse's legs as they raced to the other side.

"We heard about the fire in town," the woman said. "There was talk of a daughter, but no one knew what had happened to her or if she had perished in the fire, and for some reason, her remains were never uncovered. It's kind of a local mystery and ghost tale around here."

Mia had gone into town a few times as a teen with her parents to see a movie or to do some shopping. Her parents hadn't been turned into vampires until they were in their thirties, and though they looked young to have a teenage daughter, they didn't seem out of place with her. They hadn't moved into their house until Mia was twelve, so to the people in town she was aging normally, and her parents were aging really well.

After a few more years of living there, they would have had to move in order to avoid suspicion about their lack of aging, but no one had paid them much attention back then. They hadn't ventured into town often, and not until Mia was old enough to control herself around humans, but she'd been seen around there by a fair amount of people.

Back then, the town had been smaller than the one they'd just driven through, and she'd heard the small-town gossip even during her limited time there. She'd bet there had been a lot of speculation about the fire and what had happened to her afterward. Some may have even whispered that she'd been the one to start it.

"I wasn't home when it started." Mia had no idea why she was lying to this couple when they would erase their memories of her and David before leaving. The humans in town may not have known what she and her parents really were, but it was best if no one *ever* knew what had become of her. "By the time I got home, there was nothing I could do to help my parents. I don't know what started the fire, and I just wanted to get as far from here as possible afterward."

"It was electrical," the man said. "It started in the wall of the master bedroom and spread through the attic."

"It spread so fast." Mia closed her eyes as she recalled all the dark wood beams and the musty smelling attic. Recalled the way her parents hadn't been able to escape. Her father may have already been dead by the time Mia heard her mother's screams. "It was an old home," she murmured as her mother's cries resonated in her ears.

Mia's grasp on his hand had become bone-crushing, but David didn't try to get her to ease it. David gripped her hand within both of his, drawing her closer as her heart raced in her chest. When she opened them again, tears swam in her eyes as she gazed at the pretty farmhouse.

For a minute, Mia became so entrenched in the past that all she saw before her was a cheery yellow colonial, with red begonias lining the slate walkway. She could hear her mother's laughter as her father picked her up from where she'd been hanging laundry on the line. He spun her around before setting her on her feet and kissing her.

Mia had been petrified that the only memories she'd experience here were those of the flames consuming her home and her family. Instead, only the happy ones drifted through her mind. The warmth of her parents' love enveloped her once more as tears slid down her cheeks. She wiped them away before the brisk air could freeze them on her face.

"Would you like to come in for some coffee?" the woman offered.

"No," Mia said. "Thank you. I've seen enough here." She turned to David. "I'm ready to go home now."

David gazed at her for a minute, knowing that she meant she was ready to let go of her past for a future with him. He pulled her against his chest and held her close as he kissed the top of her head. "I will take care of their memories," he murmured.

Mia stepped away when he released her to speak with the couple. The woman grasped the man's hand as David took hold of their minds and asked them to call their children forward. The couple turned away to do as he commanded. When the children had joined them, David removed from their minds the memories of the two of them ever having been there.

When he was done with the family, David pulled Mia against his side and they walked back to his Rover. He opened the passenger side door for her, and she slid inside. Hurrying around the front, he climbed into the driver's side, started the vehicle, and turned it around before driving away from the house.

"Are you okay?" he inquired.

Mia contemplated his question. She hadn't known how she would feel after coming back. It took her a minute to realize she felt *good.* She'd faced her demons, and a weight had been lifted from her shoulders. The grief for her parents was still there, it always would be, but for the first time, she *knew* she would be able to live with it.

"Yes. Better than okay, actually," she said. "It was time to really face what happened here and to say good-bye. Time to move on." She slid closer to him and rested her head on his shoulder. "With you."

Turning his face into her hair, he kissed her head as they headed back through the town. "Maybe we should get a room somewhere for the night," she suggested as they pulled onto the highway. "It's a long drive back, and I think we could both use a break from the road."

"That sounds like a plan to me."

~

MIA FIDDLED with the brochures in the rack near the door as she waited for David to pay for their room. There was white-water rafting in the next town over, a tour of some old village, a woodshop and lumberjack tournament, and numerous stores to shop for antiques. Most of the attractions were closed now and would reopen in the spring. The winter months were not an exciting time of year in this part of rural New Hampshire, something evidenced by the fact there were only three other cars in the parking lot outside.

"Thank you," David said, taking the key from the clerk behind the counter.

Mia bit on her bottom lip when she saw it was an actual *key.* She'd spent her fair share of time in some pay-by-the-hour places over the years, and most of *them* hadn't even used a real key anymore. David pocketed the key, grabbed the backpack she'd packed in case they did decide to stop on their way home, and swung it over his shoulder.

He turned to her and slid his arm through hers before pushing the door open so they could step into the blustery night together. The wind whipped her hair away from her face and stung her cheeks as they walked down the road past the small cottages facing the parking lot. The few lights that still worked in the lanterns illuminating the way flickered with every gusting breeze.

The motel may have been a little outdated, but the cottages were adorable. Each of them was painted a bright yellow and had tiny red shutters and doors. It reminded her of a village where hobbits might reside as the doors on each cottage were smaller than normal, and so were the haphazard, square windows. It had been her idea to turn around and spend the night there after they'd already driven by it. The place enchanted her.

David pulled the key from his pocket as they walked toward the cottage they'd been given for the night. A flash of headlights in the lot drew her attention as a car pulled in. It parked near the front door of the main office, more than a couple hundred feet away from them. The flickering lights outside the office briefly illuminated the gaunt, bearded man who stepped out from behind the wheel of the car. Someone sat in the passenger seat, but she could only see their outline through the heavily tinted windows.

Something about the bearded man tugged at her memory. She tried to place him, but he was too far away and too much in shadow for her to be able to see him clearly. She sniffed the air to see if his odor might trigger her memory, but the wind blowing around her carried the man's scent away from her. She was about to take a step back toward the man when David spoke.

"Here we are."

Mia turned as David slid the key into the lock, turned it, and pushed the door open. She forgot all about the man as she bounced on her toes and eagerly waited to see inside; the outside of the cottage was adorable, and she hoped the inside didn't turn into a disappointment. David reached inside the cottage and flicked on the light switch. She laughed in delight when the room beyond was revealed.

"Definitely a place for hobbits!" she declared as she strode into the small room.

David ducked beneath the door to enter the room. "Yes, it is," he agreed and set the backpack on the floor.

His gaze ran over the cream-colored walls and double bed. To his left was a kitchenette with a fridge the size of a pizza box. Until then, he hadn't realized they made fridges so small. On top of the fridge was a TV that was even smaller in size, and the one burner stove beside the fridge sparkled in the light. The cottage may have been tiny, but it was spotless and it had Mia grinning from ear to ear.

Mia sat on the mattress and bounced experimentally on it. "Little hard."

David plopped onto the bed beside her. "We'll have to break it in and soften it then."

She giggled as she leaned against his side. "We'll do exactly that," she said before jumping to her feet. "Can you imagine the shower in this place?"

David watched her rush around the corner, her laughter filling the room when she saw the bathroom. She was so different than the woman he'd first encountered in the warehouse; so different than the woman who had been brought to the training compound. That woman had been afraid, wary of everything around her. He'd never seen her smile, let alone laugh. Now she radiated joy.

He knew she was still dealing with everything that had happened to her, but every day she smiled and laughed more. Every day she spoke of a future she never would have mentioned a month ago. He loved watching her flourish as her confidence grew and her sadness eased.

Her head popped back around the corner; her eyes danced with amusement when they met his. "I'm not sure you're going to fit in the shower," she told him.

David rose and walked toward her. "If you're in there, then I will figure out a way to fit into it." She stepped back so he could look around the corner. "Or not," he muttered when he saw the tiny stall with a simple showerhead propped over a drain. "Is that the sink?"

"Better the sink in the shower than the toilet."

"That's a statement I never thought I'd hear before. I do agree with it though."

Mia couldn't stop herself from giggling again as she stepped closer to him. She felt like a completely different woman, somehow reborn just as a new house had been reborn on the ashes of her old one. She draped her arms around his neck and rose on her toes to kiss his cheek.

"I'm so happy," she murmured.

His arms cinched around her waist, he lifted her up and carried her over to the bed. "So am I," he said as he laid her down on the mattress.

CHAPTER EIGHTEEN

DAVID'S EYES fluttered open when a scraping noise pierced through his sleep. He pulled Mia closer against him as he listened for the sound again, but all he heard was the howling of the wind and the rattling of the glass in the windows. Mia murmured something and turned into his chest. Her warm mouth settled against the hollow of his throat.

He heard nothing abnormal, yet he couldn't shake the feeling that something wasn't right. Easing himself away from Mia, he rose and tugged on his jeans before approaching the door. He couldn't make it through the door of the cottage without stooping, but he could at least stand upright inside the small building.

He'd pulled the heavy yellow drapes over the crooked window before falling asleep. Stepping beside the window, he peered around the edge of the drapes instead of pulling them back. He sniffed at the air, catching a whiff of blood on the wind.

His fangs tingled and adrenaline pulsed through his body as he retreated to the bed. Resting his hand on Mia's shoulder, he gave it a gentle shake. He placed his finger over her lips when her eyes fluttered open. Her brow furrowed as she gazed at him.

Bending down, he rested his mouth against her ear while he spoke. "Be quiet and get dressed."

Grasping the blankets, she held them against her chest as she sat up on the bed. "What is it?" she whispered.

"Something's not right."

Mia scooted off the bed and snatched her clothes from the floor, tugging on her jeans and sweater before reaching for her socks. She froze when a new scent tickled her nose. Sitting back on the bed, she sniffed at the air. A cold chill raced down her spine. For a disconcerting minute, the entire room tilted, and she was plunged back into a time when she'd worn chains.

Her chest squeezed as the sensation of those vampires sitting on her, *feeding* from her, crashed over her once more. There was no rhyming, no David to help stabilize her; she was thrown back into those days of terror too quickly to stop panic from crushing her.

David took a step toward Mia when all the color drained from her face. She stopped breathing before she wheezed in a sharp breath and her hand flew to her chest. David took hold of her shoulders as he knelt before her.

Ensnared in some memory, she didn't seem to see him as her eyes remained unfocused. He clasped hold of her chin and turned her head toward him. "Mia, what is it?"

Her shoulders heaved as she pressed closer to the heat he radiated. Despite the memories battering against her, his presence soothed some of her terror. She'd just found him, just found happiness and security again, and now she might lose it all. A vampire, maybe multiple vampires were out there, and they had come for her.

She took another deep breath of David's woodsy scent, seeking to further calm the constriction in her chest as she fought to stay focused on the here and now, on *him*. She didn't care what she had to do; she would kill any who dared to try to hurt him. She would *not* lose him.

She lowered herself to the floor before him and slid her arms around his neck, needing to hug him. "They've come to take me again." David stiffened as she murmured these words to him. His arms locked around her waist. "I smell garbage. It's how the vampires in the warehouse smelled."

Lifting Mia up, he set her on the edge of the bed. "Stay here," he whispered.

"Like hell."

Mia scrambled up behind him and hurried to her coat when he walked back toward the door. From the inside pocket, she withdrew her stake. David grabbed his own coat and pulled two stakes from its inner pockets. He also pulled out his cell phone, typed a message into it, and slid it into his pocket.

Seizing the bag she'd packed, Mia unzipped it and dug around until she uncovered the small crossbow tucked within. It was barely bigger than her hand, but it was still lethal, and she intended to use it.

David glanced over at where Mia knelt by the bag, her eyes a vibrant red. Her jaw was set in determination; anger etched her delicate features. He moved away from the window to kneel beside her again. No matter how badly he'd like to keep her out of this, he knew it would be impossible. She would fight to the death before she allowed them to place her in chains again.

"Are you going to be able to do this?" he asked her.

Her lips skimmed back to reveal her fangs. "I'll kill every one of those bastards if I have to."

David wrapped his hand around the back of her head and drew her close to kiss her forehead. "We'll let them make the first move. They most likely think we're sleeping. Stay behind me as much as possible."

He released her and rose to make his way back to stand between the window and the door. It would be impossible to keep her out of this, but he was determined to kill however many vamps were out there before they could get close to her.

Mia took up a position directly across from the door and aimed the crossbow at chest level prepared to take out the first bastard who tried to enter. This wasn't their home, so there would be no invitation necessary for the vamps out there to come inside.

As the seconds ticked into endless minutes, her hand began to cramp and sweat trickled down her back to stick her shirt to her skin. She didn't dare move a muscle as she waited, barely breathing. The vamps stalking them had to make their move before the sun rose. Vampires who killed humans for recreation, or on accident, became stronger from the kill, but they also became weaker as more restrictions were placed on them. They became increasingly vulnerable to sunlight, holy water, crucifixes, had difficulty crossing bodies of water, and with every kill, they had the increasing stench of garbage to purebred vampires.

These assholes wouldn't be able to attack them during the day, unless they planned to follow them all the way back to Maine. Her heart sank as she realized it could be a long time, if ever, if the vampires didn't attack them tonight.

She glanced at David as regret descended over her. He remained unmoving beside the door. The steady beat of his heart and his even breaths belied the lethal tension of his body. She'd just found a new family and home she loved with him. She refused to let it go.

No matter what it took, they'd kill these bastards or she'd die trying.

A noise outside brought her head back toward the door. She shifted her position as she steadied her grip on the crossbow. Before she had time to take another breath, the door of the room burst open. Splintered wood showered her from the broken frame. Mia ducked as what remained of the door soared over her head and crashed into the wall behind her with enough force to shatter the plaster and shake the building.

She almost fired the crossbow before she realized the first vamp had come in low. Jerking her hand down, she pulled the trigger. The tiny bolt whistled as it sped through the air and pierced the vampire in his forehead. He howled and flipped over onto his back. His feet kicked in the air as his hands clawed at the bolt. Another vamp appeared in the doorway, but before he could jump out of the way, David grabbed his jacket and jerked him inside.

David's handsome face was etched with ruthlessness when he drove the stake through the vamp's heart and yanked it back out. Mia caught a glimpse of the man with the beard that she'd seen earlier before he spun away from the door.

Realization that the bearded man was also a vampire dawned on her when his putrid stench hit her. A flash of memory rocked her on her feet. A picture of him heavier and laughing, blazed across her mind, but she still couldn't quite recall who he was.

Mia shook her head to clear it of the image. She could piece it all together later; they had to fight. When she saw another vamp duck away from the door, she realized the vampires hadn't been waiting to attack because they wanted to follow them somewhere. They'd been waiting for reinforcements.

David bent down and drove his stake through the heart of the vamp she'd shot, who was still kicking his feet on the floor. Yanking the bolt from the vamp's forehead, David tossed it to Mia before rising and cautiously poking his head out the door. He ducked back in time to avoid a machete that swung out of the darkness at him. The machete came so close that it glanced over his ear, drawing blood that rolled down to seep into his shirt.

Rage burst hotly through Mia at the sight of David's blood, and the knowledge that another had hurt him.

The arm holding the machete lifted up, but David lunged forward and seized the wrist before the vampire could pull back. He slammed the vamp's wrist against the doorframe and snapped his arm around. Bone cracked and splintered before it tore through skin. The vampire howled and the machete fell from his ruined hand. The knife clattered as it hit the ground.

David kept hold of the vampire as he strained to hear anything else. Two heartbeats sounded from outside, making it appear that there was only one more attacker with the vampire David held. Mia crept closer to him and toward the other side of the door. She craned her neck in order to peer outside. The vamp David held jerked in his grasp, trying to break free.

Placing his foot against the wall, David yanked the vamp around the side of the doorframe, twisted his stake in his grasp, and drove it into the man's chest. Startled brown eyes met his before the vamp collapsed next to the bodies of his brethren.

In the distance, a single set of footsteps fell heavily against the pavement as the last vamp fled. David poked his head cautiously out and peered up and down the roadway. In the distance, he saw a man fleeing toward a car parked by the office building.

"Stay here!" he barked at Mia, then plunged out the doorway after the vampire.

"David, wait!" Mia cried.

She didn't stop to think about the possibility of more vampires out there before she raced down the pavement behind him. Despite her purebred status and speed, Mia couldn't catch up to him as David's honed body and long legs steadily ate away the distance between him and the bearded man.

The vamp glanced over his shoulder and squeaked in fright as David bore down on him. The vamp's arms and legs moved faster as he ran toward the car. David would have laughed at the almost comical way the vamp ran, with a high step and arms pumping, if bloodlust hadn't been coursing so hotly through his body. He'd tear this one apart limb from limb for daring to think about taking Mia from him.

The vamp skidded around the front fender of a car and nearly went down. Jumping onto the car, David's foot dented the hood as he leapt across it. The vamp spun toward him to reveal the stake pointed toward David, aimed directly at his heart, but it was too late for him to be able to stop his forward momentum. In midair, David twisted to the side to avoid taking the stake to his chest.

He seized the collar of the vamp's jacket and yanked back. The vamp's stake drove through his arm, tearing through flesh and muscle before embedding itself against his humerus. David snarled in pain and fury as he crashed onto the ground with the man. Spinning, he pulled the vampire's body through the air, over the top of his, before smashing it into the ground with enough force to crack the pavement, and the vamp's spine.

The man howled and his arms flailed as he tried to beat against

David, but his legs remained unmoving on the ground. David seized the man's throat and clenched tight to silence his screams. The vamp's face turned florid when his air was effectively cut off. Blood spilled between David's fingers as he dug deeper to tear the man's head from his shoulders.

"David, wait!" Mia gasped as she skidded to a halt beside them. "I know him!"

David's head shot up, his grip on the vamp's throat easing as her words penetrated the haze of murderous fury pulsing through him. He looked from her to the scrawny man pinned beneath him. Close up, he could see the bits of debris stuck in the vamp's beard, the oily slickness of his hair, and the smears of dirt across his cheeks and under his eyes.

"*How* do you know him?" David demanded.

Mia glanced nervously around the motel parking lot as everything around them remained hushed. Scenting the air, she caught the coppery aroma of blood beneath the refuse stink of the vampire David held. She sensed no other vampires around them, or humans. They'd been loud enough that they should have attracted the attention of the other guests, and the hotel worker, yet no lights turned on and no one peeked their heads out to see what was going on.

"Oh," she breathed as realization sank in and her gaze fell to the man David held. "You killed them all."

The man made a gurgled noise and his eyes rolled in his head as David's fingers bit into his flesh again. Mia crept closer to inspect the vampire more closely. Her eyes narrowed as she took in his high cheekbones and brown eyes. At one time, he'd been a good fifty pounds heavier. Those brown eyes had been clear and smiling instead of glazed and bloodshot. She closed her eyes as her mind ran through the many faces she'd seen over her years on the streets, but this man went further back than that. He was from deeper within her memory.

"You had a laugh like Santa," she mumbled. "I loved it as a child."

Her eyes opened and her head canted to the side as recognition finally settled over her. "Miles," she murmured. "He was a friend of my father's. I haven't seen him since I was twelve." She lifted her head to meet David's gaze. "He had some kind of falling out with my dad shortly after we moved into the house that caught on fire. My parents never talked to me about it after."

David's hands eased further on Miles's throat. Reaching up, David yanked the stake from his arm and pressed it against Miles's chest, directly above his heart. "I'm guessing Miles here got messed up in things he shouldn't have been messed up in, and your dad told him to stay away."

David pushed down on the stake, piercing through Miles's skin until he hit the bone beyond. Miles grunted as his hands tore at David's arms, shredding his skin. David barely felt the gashes as the reassuring crunch of bone filled his ears. He'd never relished violence or killing, but he *savored* this.

"Am I right?" he demanded of Miles, then twisted the stake deeper into his flesh.

"Yes!" Miles choked out through his bruised throat.

"You're the one who turned her in to Drake and his cohorts before. You're the reason she was taken and abused," David guessed and pushed deeper. "You're mixed up in all the sketchy shit, and you knew what Drake was doing with purebreds. You sold Mia to him in exchange for drugs, or humans, or whatever it is you're hooked on. Right?" he demanded.

"Yes!" Miles wailed and stopped tearing at David's arms to grab at his hands. He tried to break David's grip on the stake, but David only pressed down harder and grinned when more bone crunched.

Miles glanced at Mia when she stepped closer. "I liked you when I was a child. I was sad when you vanished from our lives," she whispered.

"How did you find her to turn her in the first time?" David demanded.

Miles's eyes darted away from Mia to focus on the sky. David twisted the stake deeper when he didn't speak. "Answer my question!" he barked.

Miles jerked beneath him and tore away more flesh when his nails dug into David's hands. David seized one of Miles's hands and smashed it into the pavement, breaking the bones in it with a satisfying crack. Miles groaned as the fingers of his good hand continued to try to clasp the stake, but the fight suddenly went out of him and his hand fell limply to the pavement.

"It was a coincidence. I spotted her one night when she was leaving work," Miles whispered. "I remembered her from when she was young. I knew she was a purebred, and I knew they were looking and paying for purebred vamps like her. I made a phone call to some vampires I knew, and they took her the next night."

So that was how her captors had known she was a purebred and where to find her, Mia realized as her stomach rolled over. "What did you get out of it?" Mia demanded.

Miles licked his lips. "Humans," he murmured. "They had their own addictions, and I indulged in their blood to satisfy my own needs. I believed they would be enough to last me for a year, but…."

"You've killed them already." David sneered in disgust.

Mia shuddered and hugged her middle. "Are they still looking for purebreds?" she asked.

"Some are, yes," Miles muttered.

"You were going to sell me back to them," she said flatly. "That's why you came here tonight. How did you find me again?"

Miles kept his gaze focused on the sky as he replied. "Once I learned some of the purebreds had escaped, and that you were one of them, I thought you might eventually return to your old home. I didn't know it had burnt down at the time, or that a new home and new family lived there, but I decided it was still worth a shot to monitor the property.

"I put a camera up and took control of the family. They were told to call me if anyone they didn't know showed up there. The father had the boy call me when you arrived. I checked the camera and confirmed it was you. I told the boy to put the tracking device I'd left with them on your vehicle."

Horror curdled through her as she recalled Kip running around the SUV and laughing. It had seemed so innocent at the time, but it had covered nefarious intentions. Mia's head spun as she tried to process everything he was saying. "Why didn't you sell me to those vampires when I was younger?"

"I wasn't that far gone when you were a child. There was still something decent in me then. There's not anything left in me now," Miles muttered and his eyes came back to hers. "Do you still like the stars?"

Mia's breath caught in her throat at the reminder that he'd once been close enough to her family to know this about her. Unable to speak, she looked to David.

Though he'd been enjoying making Miles pay in the beginning, David found no satisfaction in driving the stake through his heart. The man was broken and pitiful, a shadow of what he should have been. Blood gurgled out of Miles's mouth and trickled down his chin; relief filled his gaze before his eyes rolled back in his head, and he went completely still.

David rose to his feet and wiped his hands on his jeans before walking over to enfold Mia in his arms. Her hands fisted in his shirt. "Are you okay?" he asked as he smoothed her hair back from her forehead.

"Yes. I… I at least have answers now as to how they found me, but I never would have guessed…. I have answers, and that's all that matters. He's dead and we have each other."

"Always," he vowed as he nuzzled her hair. "I have to get this place cleaned up, and we have to get out of here soon. We don't know if they might have called other vampires here too. I doubt they wanted to share their bounty, but we can't take that chance. I messaged Aiden. He's gathering reinforcements and coming for us, but we have to be long gone from this place before they could make it here from New York."

Mia clung to him for a moment before stepping out of the comfort of his arms. "Let's do this," she said firmly.

Together they gathered the bodies of the vampires. David took pictures of them and sent them to Aiden, so Ronan would be able to see them. Ronan, or one of his men, may know who the other vamps were, what circles they ran in, or some other information that would help them track down the vampires who were continuing to buy and sell purebreds. All Mia could remember about Miles was his first name, but Ronan may be able to come up with more information about him.

They placed the vamps' bodies inside the tiny cottage they'd rented for the night. When it came time to deal with the humans' remains, Mia stood by the Range Rover while David worked to obscure their bite wounds. She couldn't bring herself to look into the unseeing eyes of the humans who had been nothing more than innocent bystanders.

David syphoned gas from the cars in the parking lot and doused the vampires' bodies with it. The older motel had no security equipment, but he still removed his name from the blood-splattered guest registry while the dead clerk lay at his feet. After leaving the main office, he walked back to the cottage with the vampires' bodies in it, pulled out the matches he'd discovered in the office, and set the building on fire.

Flames were licking over the tiny buildings that were no longer cute to her when David stalked across the parking lot toward her. The slope of his shoulders and his pinched face spoke of his exhaustion and sadness before he drew her into his arms and held her against him.

"This is all my fault. I never should have returned to that house," she said. "We never should have stopped here for the night."

"This is *not* your fault," he said. "This is *their* fault. Those vampires were weak and twisted. You never could have seen this coming. You never could have guessed it was an old friend of your father who turned you in and would know where to possibly look for you again. There is *no* way you could have expected this."

She melted against him as she absorbed his words. She knew they were true, but she still couldn't help the tug of guilt pulling at her conscience.

"Be happy again, Mia," he whispered in her ear.

The ragged sorrow in his voice had her digging her fingers into his back. "I will be," she promised, though tears burned her eyes.

He gave her a big squeeze before releasing her and stepping back to open the door to the Rover. She slid into the passenger seat and watched while the flames leapt higher into the air as they consumed the tiny cottages. Her chest constricted and she closed her eyes against the flames, but she could still see the light of them dancing against her closed lids. No matter how much better she'd been doing, she couldn't stand the sight of those flames.

Mia opened her eyes and focused on David when he opened the driver's door. "I'm getting you out of here right now," he muttered, and jumped behind the wheel.

"I'm okay," she murmured. "I'm okay."

He grabbed her hand and squeezed it. "I know you are."

David released her to start the Rover and drove out of the parking lot. He called Aiden as he turned back the way they had come, heading toward New York. Aiden told him that Ronan would take the Rover to search it and find the tracking device. Someone was already on their way to speak with the family at the farmhouse, but David doubted the family would remember anything about their encounter with Miles. The family had simply been programmed to report to Miles when a stranger arrived, and most likely to forget it afterward too.

David kept a white-knuckled grip on the wheel as he constantly searched for someone else following them. The rising sun did little to ease his stress. While they remained in this vehicle, he wouldn't relax. He felt as if eyes followed him every step of the way, and he couldn't be sure someone else wasn't monitoring the tracking device.

He would have found and gotten rid of the thing, but Ronan wanted it untouched. David wasn't going to argue with him, not if it meant helping to finally put an end to this shit with the purebreds. Far too many of his loved ones were affected by what was happening in the vampire world now.

On the side of Interstate 84, he pulled into a rest area and parked behind a black Honda Civic. The driver's door of the Civic opened and Aiden climbed out. Brian stepped out of the passenger side. David opened his door, exited the vehicle, and walked around the front of the SUV to help Mia out. He tucked Mia protectively against his side before walking over to meet Aiden and Brian.

"You two okay?" Aiden demanded, his green eyes fierce as he scanned the parking lot.

"Yes," David said.

Aiden glanced between the two of them before nodding. "Brian's going to take the Rover. I'm coming with you two. We'll meet Lucien at another rest stop and switch vehicles again there. After that we'll meet Declan, then Killean, and then Ronan would like to talk with you both. If anyone tracked you here and tries to follow us, we'll lose them by the time we're done."

"Sounds like a plan," David said, then tossed Brian his keys. "Be careful."

"Always am," Brian replied and strode toward the Rover.

David watched as Brian pulled out of the rest area. A silver Corolla pulled out behind him, and both vehicles merged onto the highway.

"Is that one of Ronan's men?" David asked Aiden, gesturing at the Toyota.

"Yes, it's Saxon," Aiden replied. "He'll follow Brian the entire time."

David glanced around the parking lot. The sun shone brightly down on them, and humans walked back and forth to the brick building with the bathrooms, but he still felt far too exposed. "Let's get out of here."

Walking over to the Honda, David opened the back door for Mia and waited for her to climb in. He slid in next to her and closed the door. Aiden started the car, pulled out of their spot, and merged onto the highway.

"It will be a little bit of time, but you'll be able to go home again," Aiden said as he glanced at David in the rearview mirror.

"I can't wait," Mia whispered as she stared at the scenery flashing by.

EPILOGUE

Mia sat in the cradle of David's legs as she stared up at the night sky through the plate glass window of their hotel room. His warmth enveloped her, and love swelled in her chest when he bent his head to kiss her neck.

It had been a month since the incident at the motel, and tomorrow they would finally make the long journey home. She couldn't wait, but while they were still in Alaska, she hoped to get in one more viewing of the Aurora Borealis.

They'd been lucky enough to see the Northern Lights a few times over the three weeks they'd been there. It had been everything she'd dreamed it would be and more, as she'd had David standing by her side when it occurred.

She nestled closer to him just as the first wave of green light moved across the sky. She sat up in his arms, hitting him excitedly with one hand while she pointed with the other. "Look!" she cried.

"I see," David murmured, smiling as Mia's face lit with joy. She bounced in his arms as excitedly as she had the first time she'd witnessed the phenomena. All he'd wanted was for her to find happiness again after the motel, and she had. He relished every one of her smiles and excited cries as the eerie light filling the sky played over her delicate features.

Ronan and his men had no luck learning anything more from the family at the farm or the tracking device. Declan had told him it was a simple tracking device, one meant to link up with someone's phone. Most likely it had been linked to Miles's phone. However, that phone had been destroyed during David's fight with Miles.

Ronan didn't think there was any reason to believe someone else may know who Mia was, and he believed any direct threat to her had been eradicated with Miles, but David had decided she needed a break and not to return home right away. Instead, he'd arranged to bring Mia there. Deciding against airports or anywhere else public for the time being, they'd driven cross-country into Canada and continued on to Alaska. They would be driving home again too.

Knowing it was Miles who had originally turned her in eased David's fears for Mia. He couldn't wait to return to Maine, settle into their lives together, and build their home.

"I love you, Mia," he whispered.

She smiled even more radiantly when she turned to face him. "I love you too. No matter where we are, I know I'm home if you're with me."

David squeezed her in his arms as he kissed her tenderly. "So do I," he murmured against her lips.

The End.

Read on for an excerpt from Eternally Bound the first book in the spinoff to the Vampire Awakenings Series.

Eternally Bound focuses on Ronan and is now available.
Eternally Bound on Amazon: http://bit.ly/EtBdAmz

Book 7 in The Vampire Awakenings Series, *Ravaged*, will focus on Aiden. Coming 2017!

Stay in touch on updates and new releases from the author by joining the mailing list!
Mailing list for Brenda K. Davies and Erica Stevens Updates:
http://bit.ly/ESBKDNews

ETERNALLY BOUND

Ronan's gaze narrowed on the woman who emerged from the hallway to stand at the edge of the dance floor. Her silver blonde hair, dangling in a braid over her shoulder to her left breast, reflected the colors flashing over her in an array of reds, blues, and yellows. The lights played over her delicate features and lit the awe on her face as she stared at the humans.

A smile tugged at the corners of her full mouth as a group danced by close to her. Many of the people below displayed more flesh than they covered, but Ronan found his gaze riveted on her fully clothed body. She wore a pair of form-fitting black pants tucked into ankle-high, black boots. Her long black coat pushed back as she settled her hands on her hips and tilted her head to watch the crowd. Beneath the coat, she wore a black turtleneck and jeans that hugged her breasts, slender waist, and rounded hips. She looked to be a good five inches shorter than him at about five-seven.

Her smile slid away, and her hands fell from her hips as she surveyed the crowd with a far more serious eye. Then, her head tilted back, her gaze locked onto his, and he was treated to a full-on view of her striking beauty.

Ronan clenched the bar as, for the first time in centuries, lust slammed into him. The image of her naked body beneath his, moving in a sensuous dance against his sheets, caused his cock to harden.

He felt like he had when he'd been twelve and first discovering the joys of the female body, before the pleasure of sex had faded away over the many centuries of his death-filled life. He couldn't recall the last time he'd desired a woman, but he knew it had never happened this strongly before.

"Hello, Sugar," Declan purred from beside him. "I think she might make a very tasty treat."

Ronan didn't have to look at him to know Declan had also spotted the woman. In a crowd of nearly a hundred humans, she stood out as clearly as the full moon from the stars. His teeth clamped together as Declan leaned forward, his gaze intent on the woman.

"Don't," Ronan snarled, half-tempted to throw his friend over the railing.

He had no idea where the impulse had come from. He was not an easy man, he was not one who took disobedience well, but he was tolerant. He'd learned long ago that giving into anger and having a temper were pointless. However, with the way Declan was looking at her as if he could see straight through her clothes, Ronan wanted to kill him.

A dark auburn eyebrow rose as Declan's head turned slowly toward him. "Claiming her for yourself tonight?"

"We have a mission," Ronan bit out. The thick sunglasses may be shading his eyes, but he knew Declan was aware of the fact he remained focused on the woman.

"After the mission then?"

Ronan tore his attention away from the woman to look at Declan. His friend's casual air vanished, he straightened away from the railing and took an abrupt step back. Ronan's gaze was drawn back to the dance floor when the sharp stench of garbage wafted through the air.

The crowd of people flowed away from the corner as Joseph glided out of the shadows. Yet even as the humans moved away from him, the women and some of the men were drawn closer to Joseph, practically tripping over themselves to get at him. A vampire's innate ability to lure someone closer drew the humans to Joseph like flies to honey, yet their instincts told them this was no honey but a Venus Flytrap set to spring and devour them whole.

Unfortunately for these humans, their desire and Joseph's lure won out over their flight or fight instincts.

Ronan's gaze darted to the woman only twenty feet away from Joseph. His fangs burst free when he saw the woman's gaze lock on Joseph as he strolled through the crowd. Unlike the other females though, this one did not saunter toward the vampire. Instead, her eyes narrowed and her hand went to something at her side.

Ronan's eyes narrowed at the unusual reaction. The dark-haired, male hunter appeared again at the edge of the dance floor, drawing the woman's gaze to him. For a second, Ronan watched as the two locked eyes and then the male was moving toward her so fast that the humans' eyes didn't register his passing. The born hunters may not be vampires, but they certainly weren't entirely human either. The fights he'd had against them hadn't been easily won.

Ten feet before the hunter reached the woman, he stopped in the middle of the dance floor. His head swiveled and his nostrils flared as his gaze locked on Joseph. The hunter's eyes darted between the woman and Joseph before he closed the distance to the woman.

Ronan couldn't hear what they said to each other over the thumping music, but when the man grabbed the woman's arm, she yanked it away from him and planted her hands on her hips. A low growl rumbled up Ronan's throat when the man reached for her again. Joseph was right there, yet he found himself wanting to go for the hunter. To break his hand for daring to touch her when she obviously didn't welcome it.

The woman's hands moved through the air as she spoke; the man's followed suit as they faced off. Then, the crowd parted and Joseph moved within feet of them. They both stopped speaking as they focused on Joseph. Their faces filled with an intense hatred that

Ronan suspected ran deeper than just a hunter's normal animosity toward vampires.

When Joseph was out of sight, the woman and man rejoined the other hunters standing beside the floor. The woman moved with the same lethal speed as the man, confirming what she was.

"A female hunter," he murmured.

"I thought they were a myth," Declan chuckled.

"Apparently not," Ronan said as his gaze drifted back to Joseph. It didn't matter who or what the woman was, all that mattered was ending this tonight. He only hoped the hunters stayed out of his fucking way.

He didn't want to have to kill them too.

FIND THE AUTHOR

Erica Stevens/Brenda K. Davies Mailing List:
http://bit.ly/ESBKDNews

Facebook page: http://bit.ly/ESFBpage
Facebook friend: http://bit.ly/EASFrd

Erica Stevens/Brenda K. Davies Book Club:
http://bit.ly/ESBDbc

Instagram: http://bit.ly/ErStInsta
Twitter: http://bit.ly/ErStTw
Website: http://bit.ly/ESWbst
Blog: http://bit.ly/ErStBl

ABOUT THE AUTHOR

Brenda K. Davies is the USA Today Bestselling author of the Vampire Awakening Series, Alliance Series, Road to Hell Series, Hell on Earth Series, and historical romantic fiction. She also writes under the pen name, Erica Stevens. When not out with friends and family, she can be found at home with her husband, dog, and horse.

Made in the USA
Middletown, DE
06 September 2018